FINN FLANAGAN AND THE FLEDGLINGS

D1523300

The HALO Series
Book One

Kip Taylor

Dedicated to:
Michael G. Thorne
and
Philip W. Taylor,

two extraordinary middle school principals

fledgling, n.1.a young bird that has just grown the feathers needed to fly but is still dependent.2.a young and inexperienced person.

Day 1

*You have learned something.
That always feels at first as if
you had lost something.*

-H.G. Wells

Kip Taylor

Chapter 1
Hostile Encounters

If racing from life's highest point to its lowest point was an Olympic sport, tonight I'd win the gold medal.

` ` ` ` ` ` `

Dad and I are walking back to the car after demolishing a pepperoni pizza and two banana splits.

"Hey, Finny, want to practice your night driving?" he asks, dumping two keys on a lariat into my open palm.

"Heck, yeah," I say.

Then Dad says something I don't expect. "By the way, I'm buying myself a new car. Thought maybe you'd like this one."

"What?" My voice goes up an octave. "No way. You're giving me your car?"

"Don't think it means you can do whatever you want. You'll have to run errands and pick up Gran for me. It's a serious responsibility. And, you'll have to help pay for your insurance."

I elbow him in the arm. "*Okay*, Dad." Dad isn't the type to give me a lot of stuff. Since my mom died, sometimes I think he goes overboard trying not to spoil me. I shake my head. "I don't believe it."

"Believe it," he says, grinning.

I head butt him, and he grabs me by the shoulders. We wrestle for a few moments, laughing, and then I break away. I want to get to *my* car.

I've never thought about owning anything nearly this cool.

As we walk, I toss the lariat clockwise, wrapping it around my hand—a little trick I learned at my summer lifeguarding job. I flick my wrist so it wraps the other way while I think about how I can drive Garrett to school, chauffeur all my friends to the movies, even organize a trip to the beach. It's going to be a world of fun.

When we get to the car, I press the button on the key fob, listening to the familiar *wert, wert* of the opening lock. As I step off the curb to walk around to the driver's side, Dad jerks me back by my arm.

"Dad. What?"

"It's okay, son. Just get behind me."

I smell him first—body odor, stale beer, and spoiled food. He reeks. He's standing in the street next to the car. His clothes are filthy and he's holding a gun.

"Don't move," the man mumbles, pointing the gun at us with trembling hands. "Gimme your wallet." His eyes are bloodshot, red-rimmed, and his mouth twitches.

"Sure, sure, no problem. I'm getting it," Dad says. He fumbles in his back pocket. "Let's all stay calm."

The wallet slips from Dad's hand. I step

forward to catch it, but it tumbles to the ground. The jingling car keys turn the man's attention on me. He waves the gun wildly, and his grimy fingers tighten around the metal.

"Finny, get back," Dad says in a strangled voice.

"You. Shuddup," the man hisses at Dad. He keeps the gun trained on me and dives forward, plucking the wallet from the sidewalk and shoving it in his pocket. "You. Gimme them keys."

A young couple with their arms linked strolls around the corner, the street lamp like a spotlight on them as they stop to kiss. The girl glances up, tossing her blond hair, and takes in the scene. She screams.

A flash of light blinds me, and a crack like a baseball homerun thunders in my ears. My feet fly out from under me, my body slams into the pavement, and liquid bubbles into my throat. The gunman's footsteps slap, echo, and fade.

"Help. Someone call 911!" Dad screams. His voice scares me. "Finny, please stay with me," he begs. I hear the sound of ripping clothing, and I feel his hands pressing on my chest.

The face of the girl who screamed appears. I float toward her. Her hands are clapped over her mouth, and she is crying. Her earrings sparkle. I float closer. Crafted of delicate silver strands, the earrings grow larger and larger until they are all I see, swinging over her shoulders like feathery angel wings.

\ \ \ \ \ \ \

I wake in the middle of a sweat-soaking nightmare wedged into a wet crevice that stinks like a garbage dump. Burning acid scorches the skin and muscle from my bones. Only my head and feet are spared.

I open my eyes, and the feverish red eyes of some unimaginable creature glare back. Rows of mossy green teeth hover over me. The teeth clamp down and my bones snap like raw vegetables. I wish I could faint, but I feel every jolt as the creature shakes me like a rabid dog with a rope toy. Finally, its mouth opens again as it roars a deep satisfied bellow.

A light drizzle begins to fall, the drops sugar-sweet. The smell of fresh cut wood washes away the stench. The creature roars again, this time a shriek of distress and helpless rage.

It spits me out.

I fall, a stomach-churning drop.

Something catches me, and a soft, cooling blanket swaddles me. I look into the sapphire eyes of a beautiful woman, her face glowing.

Exhausted, I nestle in, and a montage of scenes flits by. —my body on a stretcher, being shoved into the back of an ambulance—a paramedic pulling Dad into the back of the ambulance by the arm—a hospital room with machines beeping—my body lying still, soaked with blood—Dad leaning over me, his face ravaged—" I can't lose you, too, Finny. I can't lose you, too."

Chapter 2
Paradox

Falling again wakes me.

I open my eyes, squinting in sunlight, and pull myself up. I pat my arms and legs to make sure they're still there. Then I take a deep breath. The air smells as fresh as a dryer sheet.

Something my old Boy Scout leader used to say flies into my head. *Always be prepared.* I search my pockets—wallet with learner's permit, five dollar bill, pack of gum and a comb. I don't feel very prepared.

I sit in the middle of a parking lot. Beyond the lot, flat-topped mountains with scrub pines scattered over their slopes wrap around a valley. Behind me is a building, and in front of me, the other end of the parking lot spills out onto a country road. A sign says Rt. 90 leads to Paradox, eleven miles away.

Where am I? The last thing I remember is walking back from dinner with my dad. Am I dreaming?

I touch the asphalt. It feels hot, and I get a whiff of oily tar.

I notice an old man, no farther than twenty yards away, standing on the shoulder of the road. He's holding an oil-stained rag, and he hunches over the open hood of a rusty pickup truck. "Hello. Excuse me, Sir?" My throat is parched, the words whispery croaks.

The old man shuffles to the driver's side of the truck and reaches in the open door to try the engine. It sputters for a moment before kicking on. He returns to the front of the truck and slams the hood.

I struggle to stand, but my legs buckle. I wave my arms and try my voice again. "Hey, Mister. Over here. Can you help me?" This time, though hoarse, I'm certain my words are loud enough to be heard.

The old man turns toward me, and cupping a hand over his eyes like a visor, he scans the mountains and the parking lot. His gaze comes to rest for a moment on the exact spot where I sit. Then he turns away, tosses the rag into the back of the truck, and climbs in the driver's side. The seat groans as he settles behind the wheel, and the door squeaks as he pulls it shut. I watch particles of dust spiral into the air from under the wheels as he pulls away.

Maybe he was deaf, but I swear he looked right at me.

My stomach contracts in pain, and my breath comes in short bursts. Memories lie just below the surface, and with them comes terror. None of this makes sense.

I squeeze my eyes shut, willing myself to wake up. I want my dad. I want my dad to come get me and take me home. *I want to go home.*

A sudden atmospheric shift and a series of pops and whines make my head throb. Two small dark objects hurtle toward me, and I duck. A limp ragdoll, arms and legs flailing, tumbles into a crumpled heap in front of me.

I scoot over. It's a girl, an unconscious girl. She might even be dead. I lean in to get a closer look, reaching for her wrist to check for a pulse.

Her eyes pop open. Adrenaline shoots through me, and I scrabble backward like a crab.

"Se non puo respirare," she rasps.

It means she can't breathe, but how do I know that? I drag myself back over, and she puts up her hand to wave me away.

At least *she* can see me.

She draws in a long loud breath of air, shakes her head and sits up. "Whew," she says. "That knocked the breath out of me."

"You speak English?" I ask.

"No." She gives me a *What's the matter with you?* look. "You speak Italian. And thank goodness. This doesn't look like home."

Okay. She thinks I'm speaking Italian, and I think she's speaking English. This *must* be a dream.

I don't know what to tell her; except I'm pretty sure she's right about one thing. We're not in Italy.

Her big brown eyes flick over the landscape. Her skin is creamy and her dark hair is pulled back in a ponytail. She reaches up, tugs the rubber band out, and when she shakes her head, glossy waves cascade over her shoulders. I know at that moment I have become what my dad calls *a goner.*

If she's part of the dream, I hope I don't wake up any time soon.

"So, do you know where we are?" she asks. "I can't seem to remember." Her eyes fill, and I realize she's about to cry.

Not *that*. I can barely hold myself together, and I don't know how to answer her question. I stare ahead like a zombie, blinking.

She leans toward me. "Do—you —know— where—we—are?" she repeats.

"I'm sorry. I don't know, but I think we're in the United States." I point in the direction of the road sign. "Eleven miles away from a town called Paradox."

She nods, and the tears slide down her cheeks.

I know it's up to me to do something here. Gramps would tell me to *buck up*. Luckily, I spot the projectiles that flew by. A perfect distraction.

I grab them, a pair of black and silver heels, and hand them over. I notice they match her clothes—black jeans, black t-shirt with silver sequins, and a silver metal rope belt. She looks like a magazine advertisement.

She clutches the shoes and cries harder, until she's sobbing, big wrenching sobs.

That was a mistake.

A pain stabs my gut like the time David Gittings sucker punched me during gym because I made fun of his haircut. Only this girl hasn't touched me. "I'm sorry," I say, feeling helpless. The shoes must really remind her of something bad. I fight an urge to crawl closer and put my arm around her. Instead, I change the subject. "What's your name?" I ask.

It works. The sobs turn to whimpers and the whimpers to a word. "Sofia."

I stick out my hand. "Sofia. I'm Finn."

She smiles, a gleam of snowy white teeth, and I realize this girl is light years out of my league. She puts

10

her hand in mine and we shake. A shiver travels up my arm.

I don't want to let go.

"Sofia," I say to hear it out loud again. "I guess we should try to find out where we are, right? I mean, we probably shouldn't sit here."

Though that would be fine with me—sitting right here with this girl and her knockout looks, not a thought about the past, not a worry about the future, might be the best thing between me and a complete freak-out.

I sigh and try my legs again. A few shaky moments later, I'm up, and I offer her my hand. She clasps it by the wrist, and I haul her to her feet.

"Let's try the door of the building," I say. "Maybe someone there can help us."

Beside me, Sofia gasps, "Wait, Finn."

I follow her frightened stare to the other side of the road, where a huge orange bobcat saunters toward us. "Oh, crap. *Run.*" I grab Sofia's arm and pull, but we don't get very far. My legs aren't ready to move that fast. I tell myself again, I'm the guy and I have to keep it together, but I don't know much about the prey of wild cats. "Sit down," I stage whisper. "If we sit completely still, maybe it won't see us."

Sofia sits so fast I can hear her teeth bang. I lower myself more slowly, and we huddle together. "Don't move," I hiss. I sure hope it isn't hungry.

The bobcat crosses the road, zigzagging across the parking lot toward us. It sniffs the ground, then the air, and its tail rocks back and forth like a baby's cradle. Somehow those lazy arcs scare me more than anything.

It passes close by, and I start to let my breath out, when it abruptly turns and its startling yellow eyes

11

meet mine. Sofia watches through her spread fingers, the same way I watch scary movies.

I wonder if that thought will be my last.

The bobcat launches straight at us, running full speed within seconds. I close my eyes and wait for the searing pain of its jagged teeth. I feel a slight vibration and inhale a musky scent. When I open my eyes, the bobcat has vanished.

"What was that?" Sofia asks, a catch in her voice and her eyes darting in all directions.

I shake my head. "I'm not sure. It's just—gone."

"But I thought the bob-a-cat knew we were here. I thought we were going to be lunch."

"I know," I say, smiling at her Italian pronunciation of bobcat. "But I think it ran right through us."

Chapter 3
Shock and Alarm

"Do you think there are snakes around here?" Sofia asks as we trudge toward the lone building, as ugly and dull as a cardboard box. It melts into the mountains like camouflage.

"Even if there were snakes, they probably couldn't see us any more than that bobcat could," I say.

Sofia shudders and grips my arm. "Oh, good, because I am more terrified of snakes than of anything."

What I tell her next is selfish, I know. Maybe if she hadn't gripped my arm like she did…"Then, again," I say. "That bobcat could have been a fluke. We are in the desert, and deserts are usually loaded with snakes."

Sofia's eyes frantically scan the ground, and she tightens her grip.

I try not to grin.

When we reach the door, I knock. We wait a

moment, but there is no answer. I grab the door knob and a jolt of electricity courses all the way to the top of my head. "Yee-*ouch*," I cry, yanking my hand back.

"Oh, no," Sofia says.

I glance over. Her face has fallen. My heart leaps as I rub my arm.

"I guess we're not getting in there," she says.

How dumb am I? She wasn't worried about me.

"I'll try again," I say, against my better judgment. I touch the knob with the tip of my index finger. I feel a slight uncomfortable tingling sensation, but I grab it anyway. No shock, but the door is shut tight. I jiggle the knob in frustration.

I shift into problem-solving mode. The parking lot is empty, and the building is locked; probably no one is even there. If we want to find some help or a safe place to stay, we're going to have to break in or walk eleven miles to Paradox in the dark. Neither sounds like fun.

I step back and survey the desert hills. It's afternoon, and the sun is turning everything into purple and brown shadows. I'm afraid we don't have much time. Whatever is out there, whether it's a bobcat, a snake, or worse, it will be more dangerous in the dark. I'll have to try a break-in.

I walk to the front window and rattle the shutters. They fasten from the inside. "Sofia," I say. "I'm going to check the rest of the building."

"I'll go with you," Sofia says, panic in her voice.

"Why don't you stay here and keep knocking on the door? I'll only be a minute."

"But what if I see a snake?" Sofia clutches my arm again, staring up at me with big brown beautiful scared eyes.

What am I thinking?

"You're right. We'll stay together," I say.

Sofia takes a deep breath, peels her hand off my arm, and straightens her shoulders. "You have a point," she says. "What if someone is inside? They might miss us while we're checking." She looks at me for a long moment. "But hurry, okay?"

"Okay." I zip around the first corner. I try two windows on the first side, two in the back, and as I shake the shutters on the last side of the building, I see movement out of the corner of my eye. I hear a *click-click-click* behind me, like clawing talons. My stomach lurches and my imagination goes berserk. I know it's a monster with shark teeth, waiting to pounce.

The smell is what puts me over the edge. The fresh air, dryer sheet scent is gone, replaced by an odor of decaying flesh, rotting meat, and the garbage dump. Something terrifying laps at the edges of my memory, and somehow I know in my heart none of this is a dream.

My breathing ragged, I yank one more time on the last set of shutters. I tear around the corner and that's when full-on panic pounds me like a hammer. Sofia is *gone*.

Chapter 4
A Wee Welcome

I'm such an *idiot*. I should never have left her alone.

I visualize foul-smelling, slimy monsters skimming over the mountains, snatching Sofia and chomping on her flesh until her blood turns the soil bright red. I spin wildly. "Sofia," I scream "*Sofia*." My voice sounds like a little girl's.

I bang on the front door. Maybe someone let her in.

No response.

I throw myself against the door half a dozen times. The sound echoes in the desert like an Indian drum. If anyone is in there, they have to hear me.

Finally, spent, I lean on the door, breathing heavily as several moments pass. I'm about to head for Paradox in a flat-out sprint when the door bursts open and I topple inside.

I flop on the floor like a fish in a cavern of darkness. When my eyes adjust, I spy a little man, no taller than four feet, looming over me. He's wearing a pin-stripe suit, a white shirt, and a bright yellow tie. His hair curls over a friendly, open face. A smile plays on his lips. Sofia stands behind him.

"I-I didn't know where you were, Sofia," I sputter. "I thought you got taken by a slith—"

"Master Flanagan," the little man says, interrupting me before I make a total fool of myself, "Miss Sofia wanted to wait for you. She certainly did. But I knew you would be along momentarily. I apologize for not getting back to the door in good time. Miss Sofia and I were getting acquainted, and I lost track of time."

The little man steps around me, leans out the door, and peers into the distance. "Let us shut this now and lock it. One never knows what may be lurking. No, out there one can never be sure one is truly safe." He slams the door and clicks the bolt into place.

Relief rushes over me, and something else, puffs of sweet clean air. I inhale. "Thanks. The smell out there was disgusting."

"What did you say?" the little man asks. He lifts an old-fashioned lantern above his head. It chases away the shadows in the room. He repeats the question.

"The putrid smell," I say. "Like dead animals or something."

The little man nods, his expression grim. "Ah, yes, the smell. Of course, it was the smell."

"Sofia, are you all right?" I ask. I stand up and take a step toward her, when it hits me. The little man called me by my last name. Sofia doesn't even know my last name. "Wait," I say. "How do you know—?"

"Your last name?" The top of his head barely reaches my belt. "Why, I know everything about you. Certainly I would. It's my job."

While I'm trying to digest how he would know everything about me, he bows, the lantern nearly crashing onto the floor. "My name is Claude. I am your greeter, a very great honor, indeed. Now, if you'll follow me, we are more pressed for time than I thought."

A greeter? A greeter for what?

"Whoa," I say, putting my hands up. "Hold on. Is Dad—is my dad here? I mean, where exactly are we? What's going on?"

The little man, Claude, waits as I stumble over my words. More air, stronger puffs this time, flows over me. There must be a fan I can't see. I feel myself relax. "How do we know we can trust you?" I ask. My words come out softer and calmer than I expect.

"Ah, yes, Master Finn. You have no reason to trust me, no reason at all," Claude replies. "But, the alternative is—" He sweeps his hand toward the door. "—out there. It may be more pleasant to come with me. I will be happy to tell you what I can."

A breeze blows.

It hasn't been long enough for me to forget the sound of clicking talons and the smell of dead animals, and I do feel safer inside.

"Finn," Sofia says. "What should we do?"

Her question brings up an unfamiliar feeling. I realize I want to protect her. "Before we go anywhere," I say, much braver than I feel, "we would really like to know what's going on."

Wind blasts. More than one fan for sure.

"I guess we should let the nice man talk," Sofia

18

says. She pulls me along, and Claude nods, lifting the lantern high again as he forges his way across the space with awkward, bowlegged strides. I follow in a daze, looking for fans.

We reach a furnished area, and Claude sets the lantern down on a low coffee table. He motions for us to sit. I almost laugh out loud. The sofa is sized for a kindergarten classroom. Sofia sits first. I squeeze beside her, my knees pretzeled up to my chin.

Claude stands before us, eye-level. "I'm sorry for the accommodations," he says. "As you can see, the couch was made for a man of, *ahem*, my stature."

Impatient questions bubble up again. "Can you tell us where we are, now?" I ask. "Have we been kidnapped? Can we call our parents?"

"Master Finn," Claude laughs, "I assure you, you have not been kidnapped."

Several more waves of air whoosh by. Annoyed, I finally get it. "What's with the fans?" I ask. "It's some kind of calming trick, isn't it?"

Claude smiles.

"Don't you feel the peace of this place, Finn?" Sofia asks.

The fans are working like a charm on her.

I grit my teeth. I want her to realize Claude is air-drugging us. And it's not only the air. Since we sat down, the light has extended from the lantern and the entire room emits a rosy glow. Feelings of peace and tranquility are fighting reason for space in my head.

Claude backs up and plops into a mini-armchair, where he lifts a tiny foot and crosses it over a tiny knee. He stares at us for a moment. "I can't believe you are here," he says. "I have waited so long."

I feel like he's talking to himself.

"But I have forgotten my manners. May I offer you something to drink? Lemonade?"

Sofia looks at me, and I realize she is waiting for me to answer. "Okay. Sure. Why not?"

Claude reaches into the air and claps his hands. A burst of sparks produce two bottles, drops of condensation glistening along the sides of the glass. He holds one out to Sofia first, and she wiggles toward it. The movement drives my knees into my chin, and I bite my tongue. I wipe a drop of blood away with my fingers.

"Finn," Sofia cries. "I'm so sorry."

"It's okay," I say, but my anxiety returns like a freight train, and it doesn't help that I'm pinned in this seat. "How did you do that?" I ask. "What is this place?"

"I'm sorry, but I'm not authorized to give you much information," Claude says, handing me the other bottle of lemonade. "I can tell you only that you have been brought here for educational purposes."

"We're at a school?" I ask, astonished. "But nobody told me I was going to a new school."

Sofia lifts her bottle to her lips.

"Wait," I say, awkwardly elbowing her. "Let me try it first."

Claude smiles at me the same way he did when I foundered at the door, and it gets on my nerves.

I take a swig from my bottle. It tastes like lemonade. It's cool and refreshing like lemonade, and I don't begin to writhe in agony or foam at the mouth. "I guess it's okay," I say.

"Why would we want to poison our students?" Claude says, one of his eyebrows shooting up.

I scowl.

Sofia drinks. "What kind of school is this?" she asks.

"It's not like any you have been to before," Claude says. "But that's for your instructors to explain."

"Well, I already go to a school," I say. "Why would I come here? Is this like a boarding school or something? Did our parents send us here?"

"Master Finn," Claude says. "I do apologize once more, but I am here only to sign you in. And that we must do before you go upstairs."

Upstairs? This is a one-story building. There is no upstairs.

"Why do we have to sign in?" Sofia asks.

"We must be sure you are who you say you are," Claude replies. "What you will be doing here is extremely important. There are those who wish to interfere with our purpose."

"But why wouldn't you know who we really are if you brought us here?" Sofia asks.

Good question. I wish I had thought of it.

Claude rubs his lip. "Master Finn, Miss Sofia, you have many good questions. I am not surprised. Perhaps you need a gesture, some small token of proof that you can trust me." He reaches into the inside pocket of his suit jacket and produces an envelope, which he hands to me.

"What's this?"

"Open it." I squeeze the sides of the envelope and a photograph pops out. Several moments pass before I can speak. "It's a picture of my mom and me, on the day she—" I lift my eyes to Claude's. "But there's no way you could have a picture of us. We were in the car *by ourselves*."

"Tap it."

21

I stare at him blankly.

"Go on."

I tap on the photo, and seconds later, my mother and I come to life, singing along with the radio. It's an old eighties song, *Don't Stop Believin'*. My mom was a great singer, a professional, and she'd been bringing me to her vocal classes since I was old enough to walk. But on this day, as we sang this song, all that ended. My mother's side of the car was struck by a drunk driver. She was killed instantly.

"You were not alone that day," Claude says. "You see, I was in the car with you."

My eyes fill with tears. What is he talking about? No one else was in the car with us. He's making me mad. "Right," I say. My voice comes out in sarcastic bursts. "You were in the car with us. Well then, why didn't you save her?"

"But I did save her, Master Finn," Claude says, speaking to me the way adults do to a small child having a temper tantrum.

"Finn," Sofia says. "I think I know what Claude is trying to say."

I shake my head. "Huh?" For a second, unbelievably, I forgot she was there.

"What I think he means is that your mother went to heaven that day. And Claude is the one who took her there."

Both of Claude's eyebrows shoot up, and he chuckles.

"What are you talking about?" I ask. I swipe at my eyes, irritated. Why do I have to think about this?

"May I try to explain?" Sofia asks.

"You may," Claude says.

"Your mother may have died that day, Finn.

22

But, I think what Claude is telling us is that she was supposed to. It was her time. And now, maybe it is our time." She turns her head toward Claude. "Right?" she asks. Claude nods.

"Our time? Our time for what?" I say, my voice rising in anger. The full force of what Sofia has said pummels me. "Are you trying to tell me we're dead?" Images of coffins, wormy graves, ghosts, blood-sucking vampires, and the walking dead fly into my head. I want to bolt, but Sofia and I are wedged into our seats like corks. "But how can we be dead? We're sitting right here. I was even bleeding a minute ago."

"Still, I think it is true, Finn. We are dead. Remember the bob-a-cat?"

I search Sofia's eyes. There is certainty in them. I remember the old man who couldn't see or hear me, and a more fleeting memory of blood and pain and the sound of a siren. I feel my teeth clench. "So—what? Is this some kind of school for ghosts? Are we going to learn to haunt people?"

Claude laughs. "No, Master Finn."

"Is this a school for magic, then?"

That might be sweet. My uncle, Mike the Magician, used to be the entertainment at all my birthday parties. He taught me lots of tricks and even a great word that I used to scare the girls in elementary school. "I'm going to cast a spell on you," I'd say. "And all your hair will fall out."

"Sure, Finn," the girls would say.

"TRANSMANIFICANDOBOBANDANCIALITY!" I'd shout. It never failed. The girls would run screaming to the teacher, certain they were going bald. I got to do it a few times before my parents put a stop to my magic career.

"No, it's not a school for magic either," Claude says, "but I can tell you nothing more, except that in order to attain entry, you must sign the register. It's down that hallway." He points to one of the two curving arches in the room. "And preferably soon. The other students are waiting."

For some reason, it makes me feel better to think that we are not the only students. "Let me get this straight. We're dead, but we're not ghosts, we have to sign in to go to some kind of school, and then we have to go upstairs in a one-story building. Do I have all that right?"

Claude laughs again. "That's about it." Then he leans forward, scrutinizing my face. "By the way, Master Finn, what happened that day? It was not your fault. Not your fault at all."

Wait. How could this man possibly know how I've felt for the past two years about my mother's death? If only I had been paying attention, I could have warned her.

I nod, keep nodding. I don't think my pea-sized brain can handle any more of this. "Okay, *okay*. I'm ready." Sofia pats me on the leg.

A terrible thought occurs to me. "But what if we're not, you know, who you think we are?"

Claude meets my eyes. A shadow flits across his face. "Then you will have to be dealt with." I don't even have time to flip out before he breaks up laughing. "But I'm not worried about that, Master Finn," he says.

He lifts his ankle from its perch on his knee and sets his foot on the floor, exiting his seat in a series of vigorous scoots. Sofia and I follow, turning sideways and banging into each other with our knees and elbows as we extract ourselves from the couch.

We walk single-file down a narrow hallway. Claude pulls a large key from a chain on his belt. The key opens a thick, scarred wooden door. Once inside, Claude sets the lantern on a hook, and it illuminates a space not much larger than a closet. Sofia and I cram in behind him. The top of my head scrapes against the ceiling.

A desk with a single drawer occupies most of the space in the room. An inkwell and pen are perched on its surface. Claude pulls open the drawer, and the scraping noise bounces off the walls. Claude draws out a small brown leather-bound book, handling it with reverence. The book is inscribed simply with the word REGISTER in gold lettering. Claude rests it on the table, opens to a page near the front, dips a pen in the inkwell, and hands the pen to Sofia.

"Will you be so kind as to sign first, Miss Sofia? Right…" He points to a spot on the page. "…here."

Sofia takes her time, forming each letter before handing the pen back.

Claude dips it once again. "Master Finn?"

I gaze at the page. I notice several other names above. They blaze in vivid color. But Sofia's name is not there. My heart sinks. Is she not supposed to be here? Is she going to have to leave?

Then, letter by letter, Sofia's name appears.

Sofia Gabriella Dinitti

I let out a huge sigh of relief, but it lasts only a moment. The time has come for my test. I scrawl my own name and hold my breath until the letters show up and my name joins the rest.

Finn Aidan Flanagan

Chapter 5
A Staircase Sonnet

"I still want to know how there can be a staircase in a one-story building," I say, as I gaze up at the steep curving steps towering into thin air.

Claude chuckles, exposing a row of miniature square white teeth that remind me of Chiclets. "You tickle my funny bone, Master Finn," he says, "but you must put aside the rules of your former life, now." He pushes us lightly, urging us up.

"Will we see you again?" Sofia asks, turning back.

"You will, indeed," Claude replies. "I'm here, whenever you need me." He bows. "I am dedicated to you."

The thought of someone being dedicated to me is more than a little weird.

"This staircase is like a piece of art, Finn," Sofia comments as we climb toward the first landing.

It's true. The staircase is spectacular with its gleaming golden banisters, elaborately chiseled spindles, and footstep grooves worn in the veined marble.

When I can finally see the top, I lean over to see how far we've come. I've counted ten stories so far, each with a small landing, and we're only about halfway there. I feel dizzy.

I'm surprised to see Claude still watching us from below. Sofia waves.

By the time we reach the top, my chest heaves and I'm using the banister to pull myself up. A set of imposing mahogany doors stands guard on the landing, and we can go no farther. Each door is covered with bas-relief carvings and imbedded with jewels. The carving of a large trunk, which looks like a pirate's treasure chest, takes up most of the left door, and I recognize several musical instruments in the wood around it.

I step back to get a better look. Jousting knights in full armor ride along the bottom of the door, and other knights, their swords drawn, line the side. But my favorite carvings are the ones at the top. They're magnificent angels with halos and unfurled wings.

I rub my arm before I reach toward one of the door handles. I hope they are not rigged with the same security as the one outside. Before I grab it, Sofia pokes me.

"Hey, Finn," she says. "Look at this. I found some writing over here."

She points, but all I see is a wavering glow, like a hologram. One second it looks like letters, and the next second, like pictures. I run my fingers over the space. "I can't really understand this, can you?" I ask.

"Yes, of course. Can't you read them? They're

27

in Italian."

Here we go again.

"Do you want me to read it to you?" Sofia asks.

It's the only way I'll ever know what it says, so I nod. "Go ahead."

Sofia clears her throat and plunges ahead.

"Are you who enter here a chosen one?
A catapult that seeks the fortress strong,
It is for you to find what must be done,
To breach the wall and slay the ready foe,
So present, past, and future lessons learn,
Embrace the elder, those who spent their might,
In purpose-given humans on the earth,
Fear not your spirit life or pending fight.
Good deeds will herald news of vast reward,
Yet evil hath a way of gaining strength,
The fight to back away or run toward,
Will keep the battle charging on at length.
For if men's souls are prized enough to save,
The faithful that attend them must be brave."

"It has someone's name written underneath. Guillaume Unferth Halldene," Sofia says. "Do you suppose that's who wrote it?"

"Maybe."

"It's a sonnet, too. Do you think it's meant for us?"

I shrug. I'm distracted and uneasy. While Sofia

was reading, I could swear I heard a harp strum.

Some of the jewels flashed, and the angel wings fluttered. But what made me feel uneasy was the glow of a set of red eyes in the wood, staring at Sofia and me. It stirs up a memory of another set of red eyes. "I'm sorry, Sofia. You'd have to read it again. I guess I wasn't listening very well."

"It's got some scary parts about evil and fighting battles and stuff."

I nod. I'm about to ask her if she saw anything while she was reading, when one of the doors bursts open and a man almost knocks us back down the stairs.

"Claude!" he screeches in my ear. He's a slender Asian in a tight suit the color of blueberries. "Oh, Clau-aude!" His hair is spiky, and he's wearing guyliner.

About ten steps down, he halts, pivots, and spots us where we still stand by the doors, slack-jawed. "Scoot. Scoot. Do you think I'm talking to hear myself talk?"

Sofia and I look at each other, wide-eyed. Then we scoot.

Chapter 6
Ascended Spirits

The doors bump shut and when I glance back, they waver like heat rising before they disappear. In front of me, a low hill covered in grass as thick as a golfer's dream leads to a small village.

It's my favorite time of day, late afternoon, when practice for whatever season's sport would be over. I'd be in the kitchen, stuffing my face with junk food and ruining my dinner. Only what I see here is nothing like the view from my kitchen window.

The twilight sky is lavender and mint, and there are mountains and forests beyond the village. A narrow street runs down the middle of two rows of thatched-roof cottages right out of a medieval history book. Any second, I expect to see knights like the ones carved on the doors clopping over the cobblestones on horseback.

Fountains are everywhere, from tiny jars to one

with ten levels of decreasing size. Many of the fountains are animal-shaped, some twirl, a few have colored water pouring over their sides, and others fizz like sparklers.

As Sofia and I pick our way through, I hear choral singing. I realize how much I have missed it since my mother died. The voices meld together in perfect harmony, and I hum along.

The door to the closest cottage opens. Light streams out, and a beautiful woman, her platinum blonde hair long and straight, emerges. Her eyes catch my attention. They are a stunning aqua blue.

"Please, come join us in Welcome Cottage," the woman calls out. She waits patiently for us to get to the porch. "How do you like the fountains?" she asks.

Before I can answer, Sofia erupts in a stream of rapid Italian. I gape at her, and my heart turns over.

Have I lost my ability to understand her?

"Thank you, Sofia," the woman says, laughing.

"You're welcome," Sofia says, speaking English again.

"You may have noticed we have a universal translator here," the woman tells me. "I guess it couldn't quite catch up with that enthusiastic declaration."

How did she know I couldn't understand?

She steps aside, and we enter a large room. Beams line the ceilings, and a wood fire burns at its opposite end. I inhale the ashy smell of the fire and something else, something exotic and flowery.

Two couches, which I figure Claude would need a stepladder to climb, face each other in a vee near the fireplace. At the widest part of the vee is a long, low, cushioned bench.

Three boys sit on one couch, and two girls sit

31

on the other. They watch us as Sofia takes a seat with the girls and I squish in beside the boys. I wonder how the giant next to me could ever have fit on Claude's couch or into the register-signing room.

The aqua-eyed woman sits on the bench, raises her index finger, and flicks it. A circle of light the size of a cotton ball wafts across the back of the room and vanishes under a door. The door opens, and three adults enter, one in a wheelchair. I'm pretty bad at guessing ages, but all the adults look to be in their late thirties somewhere around my dad's age.

The invisible chorus fades into silence, and the tinkling of the fountains ceases. The sudden silence amplifies the pops and snaps of pinecones bursting into blue-green light in the fireplace.

"I'm Rouena," the aqua-eyed woman says. "We're sorry for the mystery. I'm sure you are feeling confused. Hopefully, things will be clearer soon."

Rouena's voice mesmerizes me. It's even more clear and musical than my mom's, and she has some sort of accent which I think might be Irish. She waves her hand toward the others. "These are some of your instructors. They wanted to be here for the entire welcome ceremony, but unfortunately they cannot stay. You will have to meet them later."

A gorgeous red-haired woman waves and smiles, the one in the wheelchair nods his head, and the man in the tracksuit gives us some kind of salute before they all disappear through the back door, where I hear them talking excitedly before it closes.

At that moment, the Asian man from the staircase rushes through the front door. "Claude already knew," he says. "He is taking care of it."

"Thank you, Avery," Rouena says. "Students,

32

this is Avery. He is the school's administrative assistant."

Avery nods toward us, crosses to an ornate hutch behind the girls' couch, and takes out a crystal decanter. He pours liquid into several small glasses laid out on a tray. Then he hands us each a glass.

I examine the contents. The liquid is orange and syrupy. As I sniff it, the room abruptly shifts sideways. One of the girls yelps, dropping her glass. It falls to the floor, shattering into pieces. I spill some of my own drink down the front of my t-shirt.

"Don't mind that," Rouena says as the room shifts back upright. "Claude is simply relocating the building to a safer place."

We're inside a building? How can that be possible? I saw a *sky*.

"You have all met Claude, of course," Rouena says, gesturing with her glass.

I don't know where her glass came from. She didn't have one before the bump, and Avery is on the other side of the room. And the girl who dropped her glass has it back in her hand, too, without a sign of the glass having ever been broken.

If we're not learning magic, I can't imagine what kind of school this is.

"I'd like to propose a toast," Rouena says, "a welcome toast, to the seven of you. During the next few weeks, you will learn some amazing things, but before I can tell you where you are, or even what you are, you must remember what happened to you. This drink will bring it all back. So, please."

I hear my Dad's voice. *If your friends jumped off a cliff, would you jump, too?* I gaze at the other students. They seem unsure of what to do. If they're anything like

33

me, the bits and pieces I'm remembering aren't pleasant. Maybe they don't want to remember, either.

Rouena catches my eye, and I think I see a plea for help in her eyes. Whatever. I already drank Claude's lemonade. I toss the drink back. The liquid warms my throat and tingles all the way to the ends of my fingers and toes.

\ \ \ \ \ \ \

I'm walking with my dad. Dad says the car is mine. I play with the lariat, looping it so it wraps around my hand. He and I approach the car.

I know what's coming next, and I don't want to see it again.

The reeking gunman stands by the car, Dad drops his wallet, the keys jingle, the gun goes off, and the girl screams.

I see my dad, sitting by the hospital bed, crying. My body lies still.

\ \ \ \ \ \ \

With a deep shudder, I return to the cottage. I know for sure now that Sofia was right. I *am* dead.

It stuns me.

I'll never see my dad again. I'll never see my best friend, Garrett. I'll never get my license or drive my car. No more football or baseball. No future fame and fortune from my singing career.

I've lost everything.

I see Sofia's legs kick. She cries out and falls forward. I dive for her and keep her head from hitting the corner of the coffee table in the nick of time. "Sofia, it's me," I say. I ease her back into her seat.

"Are you okay?" She opens her eyes, blinks a couple times, and then smiles. "Finn." The way she says it makes my stomach flip-flop.

"Sofia, are you with us?" Rouena asks.

I back away and perch on the opposite couch, ready if Sofia needs me.

"Yes," Sofia says. "I remember. I know what happened to me."

"Good." Rouena turns toward the boys' couch. "Nash? What about you? Have you decided not to drink?"

Nash is on the other side of the large boy, and he has his head down, his sun-bleached hair covering most of his face. He has set his full drink back on the coffee table. His face twitches, but he doesn't say anything.

Rouena frowns. "I'm sorry, everyone. I wish there was an easier way to tell you that you have passed from your lives on earth and ascended to the spirit world." She stands and crosses to the fireplace. "If you had gone to the Light, as most other humans do when they die, you wouldn't need to remember. But here you will still have ties to your human lives."

She still hasn't told us where we are.

"And now, to tell you what you have been waiting for. Welcome to HALO school for angels," Rouena says.

Shut the front door. We're angels?

Chapter 7
Seven Deaths

It all makes sense: Claude telling me he was in the car with my mother and me, the strumming harp and the choral singing, the carvings at the top of the entrance doors. Lucky for me, I even know a little bit about angels. My mom was an obsessed collector. Ceramic, glass, wood, and even stuffed angels were all over our house. She read every book there was about angels. She believed they watched over us.

"For now, you are in a fledgling state," Rouena says. "But the seven of you will live here at HALO, one of many angel communities, where you will take classes and learn skills. When you earn your wings, you will become guardians like the rest of us."

One of the girls shoots her hand in the air. "What's HALO?"

"It's an acronym, Mallory. The Latin *Hac Angeles Largior Obligatus* is our motto. It means an angel's job is

36

to give in abundance." Rouena stands, picks up a poker, and stirs the fire before turning to us again. "And now, it's time for you to introduce yourselves. Davon?"

I lean forward to see who she's talking to. He's on the other end of the couch, nearest to the fireplace, and the first things I notice are that he's very small and he's wearing green hospital scrubs.

"I'm Davon Washington." His voice is soft. "I died of complications from sickle cell anemia. I'm fourteen. I'm glad to be here, actually. It's a relief to be out of pain."

The same girl, Mallory, waves her hand in the air again. Her hair is pulled away from her face in a stretchy headband, and she's wearing glasses and a school uniform.

"Mallory, you don't have to raise your hand," Rouena says.

"Oh, okay. Davon, right? What's sickle cell anemia?" Her accent is British.

"It's a blood disease. It makes you hurt everywhere."

Suddenly, the tan boy curses and bolts from his seat, almost knocking over the coffee table. "What's going on?" he yells, his face flushed. "Where are we? What is this crap about angels?"

I'm blown away, but not by what he says. For the first time, I see his eyes. They are the same unique piercing aqua blue as Rouena's.

"Oh, my, how rude," Avery says. He's standing behind the couch with another tray, and he steps back.

"Nash," Rouena warns.

"What if I don't believe I'm dead?" he says. "What if I don't want to be some, whatever, fledgling angel? What if I don't even believe angels exist?" His hands are squeezed into fists, and he shifts back and forth. "What if I just want to go back home and be plain old Samuel Nash Anthony?"

Rouena shakes her head. I see sympathy in her eyes. "I'm afraid that's not possible, Nash. You can't go back to earth. You have a job to do here. You are part of this group."

Nash lets it fly again. "Dude, you're kidding, right?" He looks at the rest of us. "I have a girlfriend. I have a life in California." He kicks the coffee table and curses again. "Don't any of you want to go home?"

Rouena takes a step toward Nash, but the girl sitting between Sofia and Mallory scoots around the coffee table, reaching him first. She touches his arm. "I'm Valeria," the girl says. "And, yes of course, I want to go home, more than anything." She whispers something to Davon, who gets up and moves to the other couch. Then she pulls Nash down beside her. "Tell me what happened to you." Her Spanish accent is thick. She keeps her hand on Nash's arm and holds his eyes with hers. He returns her gaze, and his body relaxes slightly.

I release my breath. I had no idea I was even holding it.

"I was driving a motorcycle. That's all I remember. I didn't have a license, but my father's friend let me drive. We were all racing, I think."

"You have to drink this," Valeria tells him. "You have to remember what happened to you." She picks up Nash's memory drink and puts it in his hand.

Nash looks at Valeria for a long moment. Then he swallows the orange drink. He blinks several times before he speaks again. "It was an accident. I landed in a ditch. They tried to save me. They tried hard, but

Dude, it was pretty bad." He shakes his head back and forth.

"Yes, I understand," Valeria says. "I saw myself dead, too, with my mother and father, and my little sister. It was carbon monoxide poisoning. We fell asleep—" A tear runs down her cheek.

"I'm sorry," Nash says. "That sucks." He breaks eye contact with Valeria and peers down at his feet.

We all get quiet.

Rouena nods toward the boy next to me. "Karl. How about you? Will you tell us a little bit about yourself?"

"Sure," Karl says.

I figure he must have fifty pounds on me.

"I have a girlfriend, as well. Tallie. She was there when I died."

I check out Nash. He doesn't even look up.

"I was playing in a rugby match. My Mum didn't like me playing in the first place. That's because I'm a musician, a pianist. She thought I might hurt my fingers." He spreads his fingers in front of him and wiggles them. Then he laughs. "But I love sports, all kinds of sports. In the end, I couldn't give them up."

I know what he means. I can't imagine not playing sports either.

"The field was muddy, and I had the ball. I slipped. Two of the big boys landed on my head. My neck twisted. It broke." He lifts up his palms in a gesture of surrender.

Mallory sticks her hand up again. "Oops." She puts it back down. "I was wondering where you were from. We have the same accent."

"Cape Town, South Africa."

Mallory nods. "That makes sense. I'm from

England. And what are you called again?"

"I'm Karl, Karl Bodden-Decker. And you're Mallory, right?"

"Right. Mallory Hall."

She asks if she can go next, and without waiting for an answer, launches into her story. "So, as I said, I'm Mallory. I remember I was on my way to the library to return a book. I'm from Cambridge. My Dad's a professor at one of the colleges there, so I've always been able to go to any of the libraries I want. I was returning some books, and I had a few more pages to read in one of them, so I was sort of reading while I was walking. Ivanhoe was getting ready to—"

"Is she going to get to the point?" Nash mumbles, loud enough for all of us to hear. He raises his head and glowers at Mallory.

She glowers back. "Like I was saying, I was reading Ivanhoe, by Sir Walter Scott." She emphasizes every word.

Nash rolls his eyes.

"I know I'm a bit daft when I'm concentrating, but this time I walked off the curb, and a car came out of nowhere. You see, we really don't have a lot of cars in the neighborhood. Most people ride bicycles because—"

"Give it up, for Pete's sake," Nash says.

"Well." Mallory pauses a moment and stares at Nash. "Fine. I got hit by a car."

"Finally," Nash says.

I try not to laugh, but some kind of snorting sound erupts from Karl's nose, Sofia giggles, and I can't help myself.

Mallory scrunches up her face and scowls at all of us. I catch Nash's eye, and to my surprise, he grins at

40

me.

"Thank you, Mallory," Rouena says. It's clear that she wants to move along. "Finn? Would you like to tell us how you got here?"

"Okay," I say. I try to be quick for Nash's sake. "I'm Finn Flanagan. I got shot by a mugger."

"Is that all?" Rouena asks.

"Yes," I say. "That pretty much did it." I wasn't trying to be smart, but Karl snickers again, and Nash flashes another grin.

"I mean is that all you want to tell us about yourself?" Rouena asks.

I wonder if she means the part after I died. The longer I sit here, the more I remember. Pain, mostly. But no one else has said anything about red-eyed monsters, and I don't want to be the only weirdo. "That's all," I say.

Rouena stares at me long enough to make me feel uncomfortable. "Well, that leaves us with Sofia," she says to me. "But, before we hear from her, let's take a break."

Rouena goes back to stoking the fireplace, and Avery sets a tray of sandwiches, drinks, and cookies on the coffee table. He gazes at Nash with the same expression of horror my mother used to get when she caught me sneaking food to the dog under the table.

"Is this more magic to make us remember stuff we want to forget?" Nash asks.

"No, it is not, young man," Avery says. Sparks fly from his eyes. "It is regular human food. I did my research. I know exactly what the seven of you liked. Hmmmph!"

"That was very kind of you," Valeria says.

"Thank you, Valeria," Avery replies, bestowing

her with a huge smile.

I notice Rouena's full glass still sits on the mantle, and neither she nor Avery takes anything to eat or drink from the tray. I remember Rouena telling us we're in a fledgling state, not guardians yet. Maybe guardian angels don't have to eat or drink. Maybe that's why Avery had to do research.

Valeria and Mallory get up when I do. I want to stretch my legs, so I step over to a window. The sun is setting, and the sky's color is almost gone. I marvel again at how we could be inside a building.

When I turn around, Karl and Davon are the only ones still eating, which is pretty funny, considering Karl is twice Davon's size. Nash is standing with Valeria, Mallory is chatting with Avery, and Sofia is alone on the couch.

I want to smack myself.

I rush over to the couch. "Can I sit here?" I ask.

She nods, and I sink beside her. "Do you want something to eat?"

"No thanks, Finn. I'm not hungry."

"How about something to drink?"

"Well, okay." Her eyes meet mine. "Thank you."

And just like that, I feel like a million bucks.

A few minutes later, we're all back in our original seats again, and Mallory wiggles her fingers in the air.

"Yes, Mallory," Rouena says.

"If we're angels, why do we still have bodies? Why do we still need to eat and drink?" she asks.

It's one of the same questions I have, except I keep forgetting to ask them.

"Good question, Mallory. It has to do with the

adjustment period. We've found that it helps with the transition to keep your body the way you remember it for a while."

"So we won't always eat and drink?" Mallory asks.

Rouena shakes her head. "Sadly, no."

Nash reacts to this by pulling the plate of cookies onto his lap and stuffing three in his mouth.

"When you're quite finished, will you pass me a biscuit then, Nash?" Mallory asks.

"What biscuits, Mallory?" Nash mumbles with his mouth full.

"What are you on about?" Mallory replies. "You're holding a whole plate of them. Rather selfishly, I would add. Didn't you ever learn to share?"

"These are called *cookies*, Mallory," Nash says. "Not biscuits."

Rouena laughs. "I guess the universal translator doesn't work in every case," she says.

"So, give us a *cookie* then, Nash," Mallory says.

Nash sends the plate skidding across the table. It flies past Mallory, headed for the floor. She opens her mouth in protest, but Davon springs from his seat, catching the plate in midair as smoothly as a dog catching a Frisbee.

"Sweet," I say.

Karl claps Davon on the back. "Well done, for a sickly boy."

Davon chuckles. He sets the cookie plate in front of Mallory.

"Let's hear from Sofia," Rouena says. "And Sofia, if you don't feel up to sharing much, that's fine."

I wonder why Rouena is so careful with Sofia.

"A photographer called me for a modeling job,"

Sofia begins. "He told me he had spoken to my agent. He also said that other girls would be at the shoot. I left my parents a note, and I took a taxi." She pauses a long time. "I should not have gone."

All I can think is how it doesn't surprise me to hear Sofia was a model.

Rouena interrupts. "It wasn't your fault, Sofia. The photographer was very powerful, very persuasive."

Sofia lifts her head. Her eyes make me think of a puppy's when it knows you're about to leave it alone.

"I was the first one to arrive. I changed into this clothing." She gazes down at her sequined t-shirt. "I asked when the other girls were coming. He told me they would be there soon, but he would take my photographs first."

She hangs her head, talking to the floor. Tears drip on the black jeans. I want to hug her. I want to wipe away her tears. "He attacked me. I tried to fight, but he was too strong." She shrugs. "The next thing I know, I am here."

Chapter 8
Home Was Never Like This

When Rouena dismisses us and we get outside, Avery takes over. "Follow me, little birds," he says. We tramp along the cobblestones between the cottages, while Avery sashays ahead.

Nash taps my shoulder, breaking into my thoughts. "Sheesh. That guy is so gay," he says.

I give him a blank look. I've known gay people all my life. After all, I did live in what my mom called a cosmopolitan city, Washington, D.C. Gavin and Patrick, friends of my parents, spent a lot of time at our house. Avery reminds me of Gavin.

Suddenly, I'm homesick.

"Hey, by the way," Nash says, still trying to get my attention. "Did I ever tell you my father was a magician?"

"Really?" I turn toward him, mildly interested. I wonder if Nash thought we were going to be studying magic at first, too.

"Yeah," Nash says. "He walked down the street and turned into a bar." He snorts.

Okay. He can be funny. I smile at him before returning to my own thoughts. One in particular nags me. Should I have said something about the red-eyed creature that tried to kill me?

Avery turns right at the end of the street, and a low, rectangular whitewashed brick building comes into view. It's different from the cottages, much more modern. "We wanted you to feel at home here. The rest of the school was built for the instructors," he says, "but we built this for you. We thought that it looked more like dormitories on earth today. What do you think?"

"Did you design it?" I ask. I'm pretty sure I know the answer.

"I did," he answers, with obvious pride. "How did you know?"

"Just a hunch." He's so much like Gavin, who was always talking about designs or taking me and my parents to different memorials and museums.

We approach through a narrow path, and Avery opens a beautiful stained-glass door. "Little birds, this is your new home. Girls reside in the right wing, boys in the left."

As we make our way through the short foyer, Karl shouts, "A piano!" He lopes across the floor to a baby grand, a shiny black colossus, and pulls out the bench. He sits, stretches his fingers over the keys, and begins to play practice scales.

I listen as Karl's fingers move up and down the piano keys. He's fast and doesn't make a single mistake.

Avery gives the rest of us the Readers Digest

version of various "homey aspects of his design," pointing out a dome, modern furnishings, the kitchen, French doors leading to a patio, a large fenced-in back yard, and a wall of game machines for us to entertain ourselves.

When Karl launches into a melody, I recognize it. He has talent. He also has what my Dad always said was the most important element of all, an "emotional connection" with the music. "Hey, wasn't that *Appassionato*?" I ask, as Karl lifts his fingers and the last notes echo.

"How did you know that? Are you a musician, too?"

"I sing," I say. "But my father was pretty much Beethoven's greatest fan. He even had a statue of Beethoven's head on his desk. Do you know *Pathetique*?"

"Sure. Piano Sonata #8 coming right up," Karl says.

"It's not a statue if it's only his head," Mallory says.

The music is hypnotic, and Mallory's words are like a fly I want to swat.

"Finn," Mallory repeats, louder.

"Huh?"

"I said it's not a statue if it's just a head. It's called a bust."

I look at her like she has *two* heads. Maybe Nash's impatience with this girl is not all his fault.

"What are you talking about, Mallory?" Nash asks, on cue. "From the neck up, it's a head. Drop it on the floor, then it's a bust."

I turn my head, but I'm sure Mallory can still tell I'm laughing.

"Hmmph," she says. "He thinks he's brilliant, doesn't he?"

Karl comes to the end of the piece's first movement, and Avery taps him on the shoulder. "Thank you, Karl," he says. "That was wonderful. However, we must get you to your rooms. You, Davon, Finn, and Nash are that way." He points to the hallway past the game wall. "I will accompany the girls to their room."

We say goodnight to the girls, and Avery's voice fades as we shuffle toward the end of our hall. On each side is a half-open door.

Davon pushes the left door open and we follow him into a bedroom with two beds, two desks, lots of shelves, and several gigantic windows. The walls are lined with colorful movie posters.

"This is definitely my room," Davon says. He pulls a bunch of magazines from a shelf and sets them on a desk. "I have collected comic books since I was— like, three. But I've never seen anything like this." He shuffles through the ones he has pulled; *Captain Marvel, Batman, Metal Men, G.I. Joe, X-Men, Superman.* he slaps his forehead and jumps up and down. "Woo hoo!" he yells. "Check it out! A Batman signature series signed by Jerry Robinson. I saw one once on eBay, but I never thought I'd ever get my hands on one. Don't know what y'all are doin' for the rest of the night." He dives on a bed, bounces up, and flips over, still holding the copy of Batman above him. "I'll be reading."

"I guess this is my room, too," Karl says. "I love movies, and there's a bunch of piano music and some rugby shirts in the closet. Seems like these angels took some time to get to know who we are."

"Let's go, Nash," I say. "I guess we're across

the hall."

We exit, and I push open the other door. What I see is totally unbelievable.

Chapter 9
Reunion with an Old Friend

"Riley!" I shout.

The room has two platform beds. Riley, my little white mutt with one brown ear, spins in circles on one of them, and he has wings! I rush over and scoop him up. He puts a paw on each of my shoulders, hugs, me, and then licks my face. When I let him go, his wings flap enough to help him float back to the bed. "Nash, it's my dog. How did they get my dog here?"

"Dude, Finn," Nash says. "That's your dog?"

"Yeah. This is Riley. He died last year." I notice a few dog toys and a dog bed in a corner. I pick up a green rubber bone and toss it. Riley heads for it, literally taking a flying leap.

"I'm happy for you," Nash says, but I do not hear happy in his voice.

Riley chews on his bone, and I take stock. Two surfboards hang above the other bed, two bicycles lean against another wall, and two desks, two bureaus, two large windows, and a closet make up the rest of the room. I gesture to the surfboards. "Those must be yours," I say.

"What's the point?" Nash replies, strolling over to the bed and eyeing the surfboards. "I bet there's no place to catch waves around here."

"Yeah, but then why would they be here? We have to have some perks, or who would want to do this fledgling thing, right?"

Nash gazes at me, and the corners of his mouth turn up a little. I feel pretty good, like maybe I've cheered him up.

It doesn't last long. He notices a framed picture from the desk, picks it up, swears loudly, and slams the frame back down on the desk, the sound of shattering glass piercing the stillness in the room.

"What's the matter?" I ask.

"It's a picture of my girlfriend. If they want me to forget about her, why did they put a picture of her in here?"

Nash throws himself face down on the bed. I cross over to the desk and pick up the picture. Through the cracks in the glass, I can see that the girl has strawberry blonde hair, and she's wearing a red and white cheerleading uniform with the letter "S" on the front. "What's her name?" I ask.

"Jordana."

"She's pretty. How'd you get her to go out with you?" I ask, still trying to lighten things up.

"Ha, ha. Tell you the truth, though, I don't know." Nash turns over and sits up. He pulls the frame out of my hands. "I miss her. What happened, man? I wasn't ready to die."

I kind of get what he means. Though I'm still in shock, I don't think I was ready to give up my life either. It would have been so much fun to drive around in my own car with all my friends.

I start to tell Nash about Dad giving me the car, but I can tell he's already forgotten about me. He's fallen back on the bed, dropping the frame beside him, and he's covered his head with a pillow. As he mutters something that sounds like, "Get out," I turn back to my side of the room, leaving him alone. Besides, that picture of Jordana reminds me of Sofia. I want to show her my dog.

I call Riley and set off down the hall. I know I'm using Nash and Riley as excuses. Sofia has only been out of my sight for a few minutes, but I'm anxious to see her again.

Chapter 10
New Friends

When I think about it, I guess I've known for a long time that Riley was an angel. Though he only weighs twelve pounds, Riley looks larger due to the fluff factor. He has long thick white hair and triangle-shaped Dumbo ears. His tail curves over his back like a feathery comma. He isn't yappy, either. I used to stuff him in my backpack and take him to places that dogs weren't allowed, and nobody would even know he was there.

Excuse or not, I can't wait for Sofia to meet him, and as I flounder in the dark great room, trying to find the girls' hallway, I remember when Dad and I found Riley, running the streets of D.C. He'd obviously been homeless for a while because he couldn't have been more dirty, skinny, or flea-infested. He was afraid of everything at first, but I took him everywhere with me, and pretty soon he was friends with all the neighborhood dogs and their families.

It didn't take long for Riley to show me his gratitude.

＼＼＼＼＼＼＼

When I was nine, in the fourth grade, only a few weeks after we brought Riley home, I was skateboarding on the sidewalk outside my house. Riley was watching me with the patience only dogs have, when my buddy Garrett walked out from between our yard and the neighbor's carrying his skateboard.

I was trying out a new move. I had my left foot riding on my skateboard and my right foot skimming the curb. Garrett set up about half a block behind me, and we decided to head down to 7-11 for a couple of Slurpees. Riley trotted along on the grass while Garrett rambled on about his family's new Wii game.

"I swear, Garrett, you always get the good stuff before I do," I whined.

Garrett's reply was drowned out by the engine noise of a truck, which I had no idea was swerving out of control right toward me.

Suddenly, Riley snagged my pants' leg in his mouth, yanking me off my board with a massive jerk. The skateboard flew down the road, and I landed hard on my knees in the grass before falling over on my side. I watched the truck zoom by, bearing down on my skateboard and splintering it into a million flying pieces. The truck's gigantic front wheels ran up the curb where a tree stopped it. The truck's horn got stuck, and as it blared, I lay there, gaping stupidly at my bloody grass-stained knees through the holes in my pants.

Garrett sprinted over. "Finn, I saw the whole thing. If Riley hadn't pulled you off your board, you'd be toast!"

"Garrett," I said. "For once in your life, you're right. Riley saved my life."

`＼ ＼ ＼ ＼ ＼ ＼ ＼`

I can barely see Riley as he trots ahead of me, but every few steps he soars in the air like a dolphin riding waves. He stops at the only door in this hallway. It's closed, but I hear murmuring voices. With Riley there to give me courage, I knock.

Mallory calls out, "Come in."

I reach for the handle, but Valeria is already opening the door. I can see that she has been crying. Over her head, I spy framed pictures spread out on one of the beds. "Whoa, I'm sorry. I'll stop by another time." I back up a step or two, but Valeria spots Riley.

"Oh, Finn. What a precious little dog. Where did you find him? What's his name?"

"Riley," I say. "He was my dog from, um, before." It's like I don't know how to refer to my life anymore.

"Come in, come in. May I pet him?" Valeria stoops in front of Riley as he promenades in, full of himself.

Mallory pops her head up from a book and squeals. "Oh! A dog. I miss my dogs. I have three. One is a Corgi. The queen has Corgis, you know. I also have a bulldog. My father likes bulldogs, but my mother wishes it didn't slobber so much—"

Mallory chatters on about her dogs, but I no longer hear her. I've spotted Sofia, who sits at a dressing table with her back to me. She waves in the mirror as I stare, entranced, while she brushes her long hair.

It occurs to me that I don't have a chance with her, not really, and then Mallory's voice sneaks back in. "Look at this shelf, too. I have several of Shakespeare's works, some Jane Austen, some Bronte, and over here, the Harry Potter series."

Sofia turns around. "Hi, Finn," she says. She tilts her head in Mallory's direction and winks at me. "Thanks for bringing your dog for us to meet. Is it a boy or a girl?"

"He's a boy."

"Riley, right? I think he is cheering Valeria." She stands and walks toward me. "Did you like your room?"

"It's okay."

"Ours is amazing, isn't it?"

I pull my eyes away from her. All the furniture is clear. It must be made out of acrylic or something, and it makes everything look like it's floating. Definitely cool. But I don't really know what to say. Decoration was never my thing. I'm more of a clothes-piled-all-over-the-floor type. "Nice," I manage.

Then I notice three oil paintings on one of the walls, each individually lighted like art in a museum. I walk closer to examine them. "These are amazing," I say.

"You like them?" Sofia says.

I nod, squinting to get a closer look. "They're spectacular."

"I painted them."

My head whips around. "You painted these?" I'm awestruck. One is a still life of fruit and flowers, another a full moon over the sea, and the last a harbor, its surrounding hills dotted with villas. "Sweet. I like this one best, I think." I point to the harbor scene.

"Yes. My family and I vacationed there every summer." I hear a wistful note in her voice.

"You have a lot of talent." I've totally forgotten that anyone else is in the room.

"Thanks." Sofia gestures toward a door on the other side of her dressing table. "If you like those, then come with me. I have something else to show you."

I nod, thinking how I would follow this girl anywhere, no problem.

She takes my hand and leads me into a room full of easels and paintings, as well as a couple futons. The windows are dark, but I know that the sunshine will pour in during the day, giving her the light that an artist needs. "This is my art studio. The angels made it just for me."

Kip Taylor

Day 2

Children have to be educated, but they have also to be left to educate themselves.

-Abbe Dimnet

Kip Taylor

Chapter 11
Angels 101

I stumble into the great room the next morning, Nash right behind me. Everyone else is awake already, and Avery must have been there because the counter is loaded with fruit, doughnuts, bacon, eggs, toast and juice. Gavin would have called it "a delightful repast."

Nash goes straight for the pinball machine, while I head for the food. I go behind the counter of the island and grab a couple pieces of toast. After I butter them, I come back around to see what everyone is doing.

Davon sits on the couch with a pile of comic books on one side and a plate full of doughnuts on the other. Riley is sitting beside him. With a flash of pink tongue, Riley licks one of the doughnuts. He checks to see if Davon notices. When Davon doesn't, Riley clenches the doughnut between his teeth, hops off the couch, and disappears into a corner behind a chair.

The little thief.

Nash bangs on the top and sides of the pinball machine and mutters to himself.

The girls perch on stools at the counter. Sofia sips a glass of juice, and I can't help it, I gawk at her. She's wearing a short skirt, and her legs cross gracefully over the bars of the stool. How am I supposed to act cool when she has legs like that?

I head toward the piano, where I lean against it and watch Karl play. "I didn't recognize that one," I say when he takes a break.

"That's because I wrote it," Karl says, grabbing his coffee cup from the top of the piano.

"Sweet." It's the word Garrett and I used to use all the time, the same way people say *you know* or *like*—a habit. I'm still doing it here. For a moment, I stagger under the weight of my homesickness. I wonder if Garrett and the rest of my friends miss me.

"Yes, you are very good," Valeria says.

Karl swivels on the piano bench and relaxes against the keys. He grips his coffee mug with both hands, making the coffee mug look like a demitasse cup.

How can anyone have hands that big?

"Thanks, Val," Karl says, smiling at her.

I can tell by the way he calls her Val he thinks she's hot. She, however, does not have on a short skirt like Sofia does.

"Did you take a lot of lessons?" Valeria asks.

"Some. But, mostly I picked it up here and there." He pushes off the bench and walks over the island counter, where he plucks an orange from the bowl of fruit and starts to peel it. He offers Valeria a piece.

The orange reminds me of the juicer my dad and I got for my mom the Christmas before she died, which makes me realize since we've been at HALO, I haven't noticed a single electronic item. No television, no computer, no appliances. The lighting fixtures have no cords. Even the games are low tech; pinball, foosball, air hockey, and chess. Nothing is plugged in.

I watch Nash shout at the pinball machine, then kick it. I think about taking him a plate of food to get him away from the game.

"I didn't hear much piano music in Mexico," Valeria says, continuing her conversation with Karl. "Mostly Latino, and some country music. That's my favorite."

"I'll see what I can do about that." Karl bites into an orange wedge, and a light mist sprays the air.

"*If music be the food of love, play on*," Mallory says from her seat, two stools down.

"So, now you're going to quote Shakespeare for us?" Nash asks. He has quit the pinball machine and is sitting on the arm of a chair. He falls back into the cushions and turns his attention to his wiggling toes.

"Spot on, Nash," Mallory says, "though I must say I didn't expect—"

Nash puts up his hand to stop her, still staring at his toes. "Don't care. Don't like school. Don't like reading." Then he looks directly at Mallory. "What are you, anyway, some kind of know-it-all?"

"Yes, as a matter of fact, I'm smart. It doesn't surprise me that you wouldn't appreciate that. You probably like stupid girls, like cheerleaders or something."

Mallory, of course, has no idea that she has said the worst possible thing.

63

Nash swings his sandaled feet around and vaults off the chair. "As a matter of fact, I do like cheerleaders," he says. He leaps at Mallory. "Rah, rah, rah!" he shouts, pushing his arms up with each syllable.

Mallory leans back on her stool, holding up her hands to fend him off, but Nash doesn't stop. He pretends to wave imaginary pom-poms while stepping side-to-side and kicking his legs, doing his own rendition of a cheer in a high-pitched falsetto voice.

*"I'm Mallory Hall, and I like Shakes-peare,
I always walk around with my nose in the air!"*

Part of me wants to laugh, and part of me fears the two of them will come to blows. Avery arrives in the nick of time, and I hear him before I see him. "Hello, little birds. Did you enjoy your delightful repast?"

I choke on my toast.

He rounds the corner in a shiny gold suit with a pink shirt and a green and pink polka-dot tie. Nash's eyes pop open, and his attention is diverted.

"Let me know if there is anything else you would like for tomorrow," Avery says. "I'm all for tweaking the menu. And now, let us fly. It's going to be such an exciting day. We don't want to be late."

I worry Nash is going to blow a gasket.

We all gather outside, where Avery tells us our schedule for the day; a class in the morning, one in the afternoon, and lunch and a rest period in between. Our first class is back at Welcome Cottage. He leads us there, down the cobblestone lane under a cloudless sky.

Once inside, we all flop on the couches, and I make sure I get a seat next to Sofia. The windows are open and the sun streams in. Riley crawls into my lap and promptly falls asleep. I pet him, absent-mindedly daydreaming about splashing around with Sofia in an Olympic-size pool.

"Have any of you ever participated in a seminar before?" Rouena asks, ripping me from my daydream as she hands out small notebooks and pencils to each of us.

Mallory raises her hand and Karl nods. I think maybe I've had a class or two where the teacher tried a seminar, but it didn't work out because there were too many students.

"Okay. Maybe someone who has participated would like to tell us more," Rouena says.

Mallory's hand goes up. "It's basically an informal discussion." She adjusts her glasses. "You only speak when you have something to contribute."

"Thanks, Mallory. That's about it. However, there are a few rules I want you to follow."

I fluff a pillow and settle back. I know about teachers and their rules.

Rouena explains about respect for each other's opinions and what to do if two people start talking at the same time. Then, she makes a point of telling us we don't have to raise our hands.

Mallory immediately raises her hand.

"Remember, Mallory. You don't have to *raise* your hand," Rouena says.

"I'm sorry. It's a habit. So, are we going to be graded?" Mallory asks.

Nash snickers.

"No, Mallory. Seminar is not graded. It's simply a way for the seven of you to learn to communicate with each other."

"I think what Mal-*aria* means is, are we going to get a report card? You know, for her straight 'A's'," says Nash.

"My name is Mallory, not malaria. Malaria is a mosquito-borne infectious disease, which is found in tropical regions—"

Nash snickers again, and I swear I can see Rouena stifling a smile before she cuts Mallory off. "One of you will be selected by each instructor to be the top student in his or her class. I guess you could view that as a grade of some sort."

Mallory raises her hand halfway, catches herself, and lowers it. "Can the same student win every time?" she asks.

"We hope not," Rouena says.

Nash sits back and shakes his head.

"Today's topic is angels," Rouena continues, leaning toward us. "I want to find out what you already know about us. The notebooks are there if you want to jot down ideas."

Angels are an easy topic for me. I had an obsessed angel-collector for a mother. I don't need to write anything down, so I watch the rest of the group. I can tell Nash always got in trouble at school. He tosses his pencil and notebook on the coffee table, fidgets, and pumps his legs up and down. His eyes dart all over the room like he's planning a prison break-out.

Mallory is the exact opposite. She closes her eyes as she concentrates, smiling to herself and pausing every once in a while to write furiously in her notebook.

Karl taps his pencil, playing a song only he can hear, and then gazes at the ceiling as if hoping some answers are inscribed up there.

Valeria folds her hands and meditates. Sofia

doodles.

Davon cracks me up. He stuffs the notebook and pencil in his pocket, and then takes out a plastic toy of a superhero with a cape. He flies it in the air a little bit below Rouena's line of sight. When he sees me catch him with it, he grins.

After a few minutes, Mallory stops writing and raises her hand.

Rouena sighs. "Go ahead, Mallory."

"Well, to begin with, angels wear long white robes. They have beautiful white wings, and they—"

"Thank you, Mallory," Rouena says, cutting her off again. "Anyone else?"

Nash raises his hand. Then he puts it down and says, "Oops, sorry. Habit."

Mallory eyes flash. "Surly, isn't he?"

I'll need a dictionary if I'm going to be around this girl.

"I do have a question," Nash says. "If angels have wings, why don't you have them?"

"Nash. I'm so glad you asked that question," Rouena answers, in a way that makes me think she really isn't. "As a matter of fact, I do have wings. You simply can't see them yet. Does that help?" She smiles sweetly.

I'm pretty sure Nash just got put in his place.

"But we can see Riley's wings," I say.

"That's because Riley is an animal. Animals go back and forth between earth and the spirit world all the time. And we are withholding our wings from you for the time being on purpose."

"Why?" Nash asks.

"They would be a distraction," Rouena says. "But, don't worry. You'll see them very soon."

"I have heard that angels can perform miracles, like healing the sick," Valeria says.

"Yes, some angels have the ability to heal," Rouena answers. "But it is a rare gift."

"Can angels play musical instruments?" Karl asks.

Mallory jumps in. "Yes, they can. Like trumpets and harps. I've seen pictures."

"And the piano, maybe?" Karl plays a few seconds of air piano on the coffee table.

"And, angels are known for singing, as well," Mallory continues, checking her notes. "I heard them when I arrived. As soon as I stepped away from the door, when I saw the fountains, I heard this choral singing—"

"I've seen some beautiful paintings of angels," Sofia says. "But I always wondered how the painters knew what they looked like."

"They can't be as good as your paintings," I gush.

Nash stares at me. I feel my face flush. It isn't the coolest thing I've ever said.

But Sofia rewards me with a dazzling smile. "Thank you, Finn."

Nash sits back, propping his feet on the coffee table, pushing it toward the other couch a little. "What I really want to know is what any of this has to do with me. Karl, you play a musical instrument. Sofia, sounds like you paint. Mal-*ady*, you're obviously a walking Wikipedia. But, um…since when do angels surf?"

An image flashes before me: white-robed angels with wings and halos, riding waves. I laugh. "Nash has a point," I say. "Why would you pick us if we don't have any kind of angel talent?"

"You may not know what your talent is yet," Rouena answers, "but that doesn't mean you don't have one."

"Sure, Finn," Sofia says. "I bet there are lots of things you and Nash can do."

Where did this girl come from?

Davon's thin voice floats over from the other end of the couch. "Angels are in the Bible, aren't they?" he says. "I mean, that's the only place I've ever heard about them, like in church and stuff." His tone is so serious, I wonder if he has been following the conversation.

"The Bible definitely portrays angels, as do other religious texts," Rouena says.

"My preacher said angels fight demons," Davon says. He sits up straight. "That's why I like comic books—because superheroes fight bad guys."

I think I see what he's getting at. His interest in comic books might have something to do with angels. I guess Davon *is* listening.

Mallory pipes up again. She tells us she's read about angels in classic and popular literature. As usual, she goes off on a tangent and my eyes glaze over.

"Time out," Nash says.

Mallory pauses mid-sentence.

"This discussion has raised a very interesting academic dilemma, and though I doubt any of you will be able to make sense of this for me, if you do have any insight, feel free to raise your hand."

I've never heard him use words this big or be so serious. Mallory's hand hovers, ready to respond first to his challenge.

"Please raise your hand if—"

Nash pauses, gazing calmly at each of us. "—you do not

69

use deodorant."

Mallory's hand shoots up before the words penetrate her brain; then she yanks it down again, her eyebrows scrunching. Meanwhile, Nash's hoots of triumph echo throughout the room.

I can't help but give the guy credit. Nash's little prank had Mallory hook, line, and sinker.

Rouena ploughs on. "How about you, Finn? You have something to share, don't you?"

All eyes turn to me. "I do know a little," I say. "My mother was a big believer in angels. She was convinced angels were all around us, protecting us whenever we needed it."

"Did you believe?" Sofia asks.

"I never thought much about it," I say. "I guess I did, until—" A stabbing pain in my stomach stops me.

"Good job, everyone," Rouena says. "I can hardly believe for most of you this was your first seminar. Now, why don't you go have some fun? Explore the grounds and get some exercise or something."

I hang back a moment as everyone leaves.

"Thanks, Rouena," I say. "I don't like talking about my mom."

"I know, Finn—and, you're welcome." Smiling, she waves me away.

Chapter 12
Ride With a Roommate

Mallory and Valeria settle in the great room to listen to Karl play the piano, Davon goes to his room to read comic books, and Sofia retreats to her studio to paint.

I'm restless. I need some physical activity. I ask Nash if he wants to go for a bike ride.

"Finn for the win!" he shouts.

We grab the bicycles from our room and maneuver them down the narrow hallway. I hear the echo of my parents. *Wear a helmet.* I give it right back. What's the point? I'm already dead.

We wheel through the great room, and Karl's music pulls at me. I wonder if this is another piece he wrote.

Riley and I stroll along a lake. The fragrance of orange blossom wafts by as I pick up a stick. "Go get it, Riley. Good boy," I say. I throw the stick, and Riley sprints away.

I feel a jab in my upper arm. "Hey, Finn. Answer me."

"Huh? Oh, sorry, Nash. Did you say something?"

"I've been saying your name for the past minute. What's the matter with you?"

I've been zoning out to Karl's music. Weird.

We roll our bikes out the front door. I think Riley is right behind me, but when I look back, he has found a soft spot on Valeria's lap, and his eyes say, *See ya later chump*.

The little traitor.

Nash and I pedal over to the village, where I hop off to walk my bike across the street. Nash war-whoops over the cobblestones, bumping up and down, and I laugh when he nearly gets thrown off.

I glance at the flowering pots in the window of the nearest cottage. The glass is old, thick and wavy, and the flowers look like they're bending in a breeze. As I pass, the flowers change colors like horses in the city of Oz. Another window is full of books and magazines, piled high. A bird and a cat sit together in front of the stack. The bird is eating seeds, and the cat nuzzles against it.

I climb back on the bike and follow Nash. We pick up speed on a wide hard-packed dirt road and head toward a pine forest.

Beyond the forest is a jagged mountain, sprinkled with large black and gray rock formations. It reminds me of New York State, where my grandparents used to take me on summer vacation when I was little. Even the air is more brisk. I think of Rouena telling us we were being moved for safety. Claude must be a very powerful angel if he can move all this.

After about fifteen minutes or so of hard riding, Nash and I stop. Neither of us breathes hard or has broken a sweat. We set our bikes on the ground and sit with our backs against the same pine tree.

I wrap my arms around my knees. Nash unhooks a water bottle strapped to the bike and drinks. "Dude," he says. "You must think I'm a real jerk."

I shrug. "Not really. You don't want to be here. I get that."

An image comes to me. My dad is wrapping my ankle for a baseball game, but the image is already blurry around the edges, and I'm struck by the fear that I'll forget what he looks like. "Sometimes I feel that way, too," I say.

"I'm having a hard time wrapping my head around the whole angel thing," Nash says. He swigs more water.

"Yeah, I sorta noticed," I say, grinning.

"Why us, though," he asks. "I don't like responsibility, man. I'm terrible at it. Ask my girlfriend." He smacks his forehead. "I mean—Dude. You know what I mean."

"Yeah, but I haven't noticed a whole lot of responsibility, so far. Maybe it won't be that bad. Maybe you could enjoy the benefits for now. I mean, there's great food, a nice place to live, good-looking women." I realize my mistake as soon as I make it.

"The only good-looking woman I care about is Jordana. And I'll never see her again."

"Sorry." I'm not sure what else to say. I don't want to screw up any more.

"At least you know the feeling," Nash says.

"What?" I scratch my arm.

"Sofia."

73

My stomach contracts. "Sofia?" I squeak.

"Yeah. You feel the same way about Sofia as I do about Jordana."

Crap. Is it that obvious? I wrack my brain for a topic to change the subject. "Hey, can I get some of that water?" I say.

Nash hands me the bottle, and I take my time drinking. The only thing I can think about is whether everyone else knows how I feel about Sofia, and whether Sofia knows. Girls hate it when you're not cool, and that would not be cool. Definitely not cool.

"I've got to find a way to bail," Nash says.

Uh, oh. This is not good.

I stare into the pine trees. The pinecones, even the ones lying on the ground around us, are like fiber-optic Christmas tree lights, phosphorescent and surreal, and way more impressive than a regular forest. I can't believe I didn't notice them before. Maybe I can use them to distract Nash.

I pick up one of the pinecones and rub it between my palms so it twirls. "These are awesome, aren't they? Bet I can throw one farther than you."

Nash picks up a cone. "You're on," he says.

We stand up and decide to throw at the same time. I have a pretty strong arm, but Nash's cone goes about ten feet farther than mine.

"Okay, let's try accuracy," I challenge. "See that tree, the one about thirty yards away next to the road? Bet I can hit it right where that first branch comes out."

"Easy peasy," says Nash. He throws another pinecone, but it misses the tree by a few inches. Mine hits dead on-target.

"Okay, we're even," Nash laughs. "Let's go back now."

I'm feeling pretty good, like I've managed to lighten him up. Nash tugs on his bike, pulling it away from the tree. He scrapes his foot on the pedal and swings his leg over the seat.

"Hey, wait up," I say.

"I only want to apologize, you know," he says.

"Apologize?" I don't want to go down the Jordana road again, so I deliberately misunderstand him. "For what, dying?" I brush dirt off my pants. "You couldn't help that."

Nash shakes his head. "I was so stupid. Jordana kept telling me not to hang around with those guys. She never liked them. She said they'd get me in trouble."

"Who were you hanging around with?" I turn my bike around.

"The Fiends—a motorcycle gang out of San Diego."

"A motorcycle gang?" I can't imagine my father letting me get anywhere near a motorcycle gang, or any gang for that matter.

Nash chuckles. "Yeah. I wasn't really a member yet. A friend of my dad's got me into it. My dad's drug dealer, actually."

I digest that tidbit as I climb on the bike and push it forward. Nash's dad was a drug addict?

Nash gazes back at me. "So, what do *you* think we're here for?"

"I don't know, Nash, but I would think it's for a good reason. I mean, they wouldn't have brought us here if we weren't ready, right?"

"I'm not ready," Nash replies.

Does he think this is new information?

"Yeah, I know. I think everybody knows." I grin. "But, seriously, I guess we're going to have wait and see," I say, sounding like my father. "The good news is we won't have to worry about anything but our classes anytime soon."

Note to self— How wrong can a person be?

Chapter 13
Getting Off Topic

Avery drops us off at a cottage called Past House on the main street. We cram into two rows of seats, and our professor introduces himself.

"Welcome. I am Professor Guillaume," he says. He dresses how I imagine a college professor would, in a tweed jacket with a pipe peeking out of the pocket. "I'm your Instructor of Angel History and Keeper of the Artifacts. Today I'm going to tell you about the history of angels, a topic I believe you will find fascinating."

"Not," Nash mumbles.

Past House resembles a museum more than a classroom. Paintings cover the four walls, sculptures are set atop pillars, and large leather bound books lie open on small tables. The afternoon sun is blocked by heavy velvet curtains at the windows, but that makes sense to me. I'm pretty sure artifacts deteriorate in the light.

Something about Professor Guillaume reminds me of my math teacher in the seventh grade, Mr. Bainbridge. Mr. B. was always going on about how fascinating math was; he actually enjoyed teaching a bunch of rowdy twelve-year-olds. But his walls were covered with cartoons, not paintings.

I remember one cartoon where a man in an airport was being led away in handcuffs by a security guard. The caption said, "Sir, we found a slide rule, compass, and calculator in your luggage. You are being charged with carrying weapons of math instruction."

Hee, hee. I loved that one.

Professor Guillaume gets my attention when he hands us each a can of soda and a bag of candy. I have to admit, chomping on a Twizzler, I listen a lot better.

"In Greek, the word 'angel' means messenger," the professor says. He stands beside Nash, holding a rectangular piece of stone in his hands. "These are Sumerian hieroglyphs from 3,000 B.C. The Sumerians thought that angels ran errands for the gods." He hands the stone to Nash. "You may pass this along."

"Oops," Nash says, pretending the stone is slipping from his hands.

"I do not find that funny, young man. The objects in here are fragile and priceless."

Nash turns to me, mocking the professor. *I do not find that funny, young man.* Then, with glee, he pokes Mallory in the back and hands the stone to her. Mallory cradles it in both palms and scrutinizes every inch.

This class could end up being a disaster.

"Mallory," Professor Guillaume says, clearly aware of which member of his audience is the smartest and most interested, "you may also enjoy the sculptures and carvings from the Assyrian and Babylonian times, circa 900 B.C. Most are housed in the British Museum in London or the Metropolitan Museum in New York."

Mallory passes the stone to Davon, who hefts it like he's trying to see what kind of weapon it would make. Davon passes it to Karl.

Next, Professor Guillaume points to a couple of the pillars. "As you can see, this sculpture has a human head and this one the head of an eagle. Both have wings. The ancient people regarded these as angels, protective spirits who guarded their palaces from evil influences."

Striding over to a long table, the professor picks up a large piece of twisted metal. "Some ancient humans even believed that angels were aliens, since they came from the sky."

Davon raises his hand.

"Yes, Davon?" Professor Guillaume asks.

"I saw a UFO once."

"I'm sure," Nash says, sarcastically.

"I did." Davon shrugs.

"Get real."

"It was cool."

Nash stares at Davon for a long moment. Then he nods. It would be nice if Mallory could learn something from Davon's way of dealing with Nash.

Professor Guillaume pauses to study us. "Any questions so far?" he asks.

Not being a history buff, I've found this pretty boring, so I'm not going to ask anything that makes him go into further detail. But Mallory, of course, does. Who knew she would discover the fatal flaw, that weakness every teacher has—getting *off topic!*

"Professor Guillaume," Mallory says. "Are we going to be like the angels mentioned in the Bible?"

At first, I don't know where this question comes from. Then I notice Mallory sits next to a table stacked with books, and she is holding a copy of the Bible in her hands.

The professor smiles, and soon all the boring history stuff goes out the window. "Mallory, what a wonderful question, and a very important one. Angels appear from the earliest books of the Bible, but they are an essential part of many religions." He strides to the stack of books, searches in the piles for a moment, picks out four more books, and then spreads them across the empty space in front of the stacks. "These are also examples of religious tomes which contain mention of angels."

Mallory looks ready to burst. She reaches for one of the books the professor has chosen.

"What you as fledglings must realize is that it doesn't matter what religion humans practice. Angels exist to protect all humanity from evil."

I sit up in my uncomfortable wooden chair, almost dumping my soda on the desk. "Wait," I say. "Are you saying that angels are with every human?" In my time on earth, short as it was, I remember thinking I saw plenty of people in need of protection by angels who weren't getting it. And, if you watched the news, whole countries seemed to be left out of the loop.

Professor Guillaume takes his pipe out of his pocket, bobbing it up and down as he emphasizes his words. "Ah, Finn, we wish. But there are far more humans than there are angels. We work hard to save as many souls as we possibly can. My point is simply that it doesn't matter whether they are young or old, black, white or red, sick or healthy, Catholic or Jewish."

"It sounds difficult," Valeria says.

"It sounds impossible," Nash adds in a sullen voice.

"Not impossible, Nash, but yes, Valeria, very difficult. A challenge. We are thwarted at all turns by demons, humans whose souls have been taken by the darkness before we could intercede. Demons are our enemies." The professor pockets his pipe. "Let me show you something."

The professor pulls a small table over to the front of the room. He wiggles his index finger, and half the room grows bright, while the other half of the room darkens. The split falls exactly down the middle of the table. He retrieves a small stone from his desk drawer, which he sets it on the lighted side. "Come up to the table, ladies and gentlemen. I have a demonstration for you."

We gather around.

This is great. I love it when teachers let us get out of our seats.

"When a soul is on the side of Light, it shines like this," Professor Guillaume announces.

I see five points of light shoot from the stone, like a star sapphire.

"Feel it." The stone is warm.

Then the professor places the stone somewhere in the middle of the dark half. It vanishes. "When a human soul is stolen by a demon, the light of its soul vanishes. It goes to the side of Darkness and becomes a demon." He waves his hand over the table. "Now, see if you can find the stone."

We all lean in, our heads almost touching, and I squint, straining to see. At first, there is nothing, but after my eyes adjust, I see a faint red gleam in the shape of the stone.

"The eyes of a demon glow red," the professor says. His voice makes the hairs on the back of my neck stand up.

"Is that how we will be able to recognize them?" Mallory asks.

Professor Guillaume nods. "That is one way. Another—" He pauses abruptly, staring at us as if seeing us for the first time. "Hmmm—" he murmurs. "Time to return to your seats."

Someone groans, we shuffle back to our seats, and the professor returns the room to its original dim lighting. "What a clever group of fledglings you are," he says. "I did not plan to discuss this today. You have many more lessons to learn before you will be ready to identify demons. But, all is not lost. We still have half an hour or so before class ends."

More groans, except Mallory, who doesn't seem to care what we talk about, as long as she is learning something.

"History is stupid," Nash blurts. He legs are jiggling up and down like engine pistons again.

Professor Guillaume plucks his pipe out and waves it in Nash's direction. "Young man, have you never heard the saying, 'Those who fail to learn from history are doomed to repeat it?'"

Nash slumps in his seat. "Dude. I hate school."

The last half hour of class crawls by compared to the first half, and throughout the dark room, I imagine demons staring out at us, their eyes glowing red.

Chapter 14
First Dream

I don't remember dreaming the first night at HALO. I must have been too exhausted. But tonight, all the discussions of the day play out in my mind, blending together to form the perfect storm, an intense terrorizing nightmare.

At first, nothing makes sense, of course. Dreams rarely do. All seven of us fledglings are crowded together in Claude's room downstairs.

Karl's piano is there, and he's playing. Part of Sofia's art studio is on top of the piano, and she's painting. Valeria sits on the floor with Riley. She has a stethoscope around her neck and she's listening to Riley's heartbeat.

But none of that is the creepy part. The creepy part is that I can physically feel the power running through Karl's fingers as he plays. I can see the details Sofia wants to paint before she dabs the canvas with her brush. I can even hear Riley's heartbeat through the stethoscope.

It's as if I am me *and* them.

Davon has on a superhero cape, and he runs around near the dark edge of the room, waving a sword. I feel the rush of air with every swipe. Mallory reads something out loud. It sounds like a foreign language and like English at the same time, and I understand both.

Nash sits in the tiny sofa with Claude, their heads close together. They are talking about something serious, but I feel Nash block me from hearing the actual words.

All the instructors arrive— Rouena, Professor Guillaume, and the ones I don't yet know. They are dressed in white robes, their silhouettes like a child's smudged drawing, and they shimmer with color. Taking seats along a dark wall, each opens a window-size hole with circular hand movements. Scenes play out in each of the windows. They are watching humans on earth.

I'm the only one who isn't busy doing something, but the others' experiences ping off me like phone signals from cell towers, and my senses feel invaded.

I have something important to tell them. *It's life or death.*

I stand in front of Sofia and Karl, waving my arms. I try to grab Davon. I shake Claude and Nash. No one sees me. No one feels me. It's like I'm not there.

I raise my voice, shouting at all of them. What I have to say becomes even more urgent. I have to warn everyone. I have to tell them to get to safety.

From out of the darkness, shadowy shapes slip into the room. They glow a deep blood red. I run to Sofia and stand in front of her to protect her.

The shadows come closer and closer until they climb on top of me and push on my chest so I can't breathe. I struggle to wake, and when I open my eyes, Riley's face is inches from mine. He has his paws on my chest, and he's barking in short, excited yips.

I gasp for air, my heart pounding. Then I lean over the side of the bed and vomit.

Kip Taylor

Day 3

I saw the angel in the stone and carved to set it free.

-Michelangelo

Kip Taylor

Chapter 15
A Lesson in Angel Warfare

It's the morning of our third day here, and the seven of us are meeting for a class in the clearing behind our dormitory. We stand in a semi-circle. In front of me, Riley rolls back and forth in the grass, waving his legs in the air. It is another spectacular day, and I'm happy to be outside.

The other night, this instructor was wearing a warm-up suit like a gym teacher. Today, he has traded the suit for a black turban, a blue cape, and a long green tunic tied with a rope belt. He has a short, wiry beard, and I notice for the first time how his forehead, neck, and forearms are covered with small dotted tattoos, almost imperceptible against his dark skin. "Theo," he says. "I am your Instructor of Angel Warfare and Keeper of Bequests. Today we shall learn something practical to fight our enemies."

"Woo hoo!" yells Davon.

"What's a bequest?" Mallory asks. She has the small notebook and pencil from seminar, and she is taking notes.

"Ah, Mallory," Theo says. "I have heard of your love of learning."

"More like her love of being annoying," Nash says.

Theo smiles. "A bequest is something each of you will receive from one of us; a gift to assist you in your work."

This professor is more athletic and energetic than Rouena or Professor Guillaume. He moves around a lot, jabbing the air when he talks. I watch as he threads his fingers together, turns his hands inside out, and cracks his knuckles in a series of loud pops. "Now, if there are no other questions, I will begin."

"Good luck with that," Nash says.

Theo nods and smiles again. "One of the most important things you should know about demons is that they are capable of attaching to you and draining away your power. Think of leeches sucking blood. And since, as fledglings you are without wings to get away, you must be capable of illusion. The demon must be unable to find you."

Mallory sticks her pencil behind her ear and raises her hand. "Excuse me, Professor Theo, I did think of another question. I was wondering about your outfit. Is this something we are going to have to wear?"

"Let the man talk, Mal-*content*," Nash says.

"It's Mal-*lory*," Mallory says. "A malcontent is a chronically dissatisfied person."

"Make my point," Nash says.

Theo tells us that he is wearing authentic Moorish garb.

"In case anyone was wondering," Mallory says. "The Moors were the predecessors of the present day Muslims. They were known as fierce warriors."

"In case anyone was wondering," Nash says. "Someone who thinks she's the teacher here should zip it."

Something draws my attention out on the lake, and I tune out. A duck drags its webbed feet under the surface of the water, squawking as it glides. On the opposite bank, a large A-frame cabin overlooks the lake. It reminds me of a place Mom, Dad, and I stayed the summer before her accident. The morning sun glints off the cabin's floor-to-ceiling windows like a lighthouse signal, hypnotizing me. A woman stands at the window, watching us. She looks a lot like my mother. I imagine her in the kitchen, making my favorite dessert, strawberry shortcake. My mouth waters.

"Are we just learning defense skills?" Davon asks, pulling me back from my daydream.

I pat the pocket of my jeans to make sure Claude's photograph of my mom is still there.

"I want to know if maybe we'll get to learn any battle strategies. I had all the video games about battle strategies, and I could always go to the highest level. I bet I could do them here, too."

For Davon, this is like a monolog.

Theo cracks the biggest smile yet. "We'll start with defense, Davon; a basic angel strategy. It is a maneuver called shielding. But don't worry, we will learn many strategies for battle as well."

Mallory interrupts. "Excuse me, Theo, but will there be a test on this shielding?"

"Here's a test, Mal-*formation*," Nash says. "How

long can you keep quiet?"

Mallory's mouth drops open.

Theo motions for us to sit. Then he addresses Mallory's question. "The only test is that you master the skill, although whoever does the best today will receive a special surprise from me. But first, a demonstration." He sticks the fingers of his right hand in his mouth and whistles. "Riley! Come here, boy."

Riley gets up, and with a sweep of his tail, promenades over to a small tree. I expect him to lift his leg and squirt pee on the bark. Instead, he pushes against it and disappears.

"What—How?" I'm flabbergasted.

"Way to go, Riley," Valeria yells, clapping.

"No way," I shake my head. "Riley knows how to do this?"

Theo turns to me. "Awesome, isn't he?" He grins. "And now I will need a human volunteer."

Davon's hand shoots up. "Pick me!"

I can't believe his hand went up before Mallory's.

Theo chuckles. "All right, Davon. Come on up."

Davon bounds over to Theo, cutting the air with karate chops and yelling, "Hi-*ya*!"

"Go Davon," Karl shouts.

I overhear Sofia whisper to Valeria, "He's funny."

"Davon, I want you to stand by that tree, please," Theo says.

"You mean the same one as Riley?"

"Yes." Theo cups his hands around his mouth. "Riley, you can come out now, boy."

Riley's little white face pokes out; then his huge

ears. He wiggles them, and we all crack up. Finally, he pops the rest of the way out and trots to me. He lies back down as if disappearing into a tree is an everyday occurrence for him.

"Okay, Davon," Theo says. "Place as much of your body as possible against the trunk." Davon stands on his tiptoes and bends his neck, resting it against the bark. "Now, I want you to push," Theo says. "And while you're pushing, think of yourself as part of the tree."

"Think of myself as part of the tree," Davon repeats.

"You should start to feel a tingling sensation. Do you feel it?"

"I think so."

We watch as Davon's body begins to disappear like water soaking into dry soil. Soon, all we can see are his blinking eyes.

"How do I dow whed I'b id?" Davon asks.

"You're already in. Now you have to close your eyes. The eyes," he tells the rest of us, "as you may or may not already know, are the windows of the soul. They will give you away unless you close them."

Davon shuts his eyes. Theo stretches his hand toward the tree, as proud as a magician who has made his assistant vanish. "Voila!" he says. "Davon is now invisible to demons."

"Dith ith cothy," says a muffled voice from the tree.

Sofia and Valeria giggle.

Mallory raises her hand. "Does it only work with trees?" she asks.

"No," Theo says. He turns toward the tree. "Davon, you may come out now. Dig your feet in, punch out with your arms, and jump."

Davon's bony hands appear, and then the rest of him bursts through.

"Shielding works with any inanimate object, Mallory, provided the object is large enough," Theo says.

"Can more than one of us shield together in the same object?" I ask. I have no idea where the question comes from, and I don't like the premonition of danger that comes with it.

"What an excellent question, Finn. Yes, but the less space there is, the more uncomfortable you will be. Each of us gives off an electrical energy which takes up a certain amount of space. The molecules of the inanimate object must separate in order to make room for that energy."

I nod. It sounds like basic science to me, something I can understand.

Theo barks an order. "And now the rest of you must try to shield. We'll go to the back yard behind the dormitory where there is more to work with." He opens the gate, and we troop into the back yard, which is full of patio furniture, bushes, more of Rouena's fountains, and several trees.

At first, I hear the clamor of the others banging off surfaces. By my tenth try, I'm almost ready to give up. How did Davon learn to do it so fast?

Finally, I shield in a fountain, and only Valeria is left. I hear Theo tell her to relax. "What do you mean?" she asks. "How do I relax?" She sounds like I felt a moment before, completely frustrated.

"Think of it like a pillow, Valeria." I'm surprised to hear Nash's voice. "Rest your head against it. Then sink into it like you're going to fall asleep."

What a great idea. It's exactly the type of thing to imagine. How did Nash come up with it?

Valeria shields.

It has taken over an hour, but at last we have all done it at least once. Theo congratulates us. We come out of our places. I'm exhausted. Davon continues to pop in and out with ease, the clear star.

We regroup outside the fence where a large wooden trunk sits in the clearing. I recognize its ornate metal lock and decorations immediately.

"Hey, Sofia," I say. "That looks like the trunk carved on the entrance doors, doesn't it?"

"I don't remember," she says. "I was reading the sonnet."

Theo asks for our attention. "Please sit," he says, flipping the trunk lid open. It bounces up and down, squeaking loudly. "Except you, Davon. Would you please come forward?"

Davon scrambles toward the trunk, standing next to Theo, who positions him to face the rest of us. "Fantastic job, fledglings," Theo says. "I'm very proud of all of you. However, I think we can all agree that Davon was the most proficient student of the day."

We all clap and cheer.

"This is the Trunk of Kings. It is where we keep our most valuable possessions." Theo reaches into the trunk and takes out a sleeveless silver shirt. It looks like hundreds of soda can tops fastened together. "Davon, not only were you able to master the art of shielding with no problem, but you show the most interest in learning about warfare. Therefore, this item is for you."

Theo helps Davon fit the silver shirt over his head. It glistens in the sun like sardines swimming in a stream.

"Wow," Davon says. The shirt is so large, it falls to his knees. "This is armor, isn't it?"

"It is called a hauberk," Theo says. "It's one of the types of armor worn by knights during the middle ages."

"Yeah, the knights wear something exactly like this in Teutonic Tactics, my favorite video game."

"Yes, but the Teutonic knights were warriors. This hauberk belonged to a peace-loving Moor. It was mainly for defensive purposes."

"That's cool," Davon says. "Defensive strategies are my favorite."

"The Moor's name was Theodopolous," Theo says.

"Theodopo—Theo? You mean, this was yours?" Davon's eyes open wide.

"Yes, it should protect you from harm, enabling you to be front and center during a battle."

"Thanks, Theo." Davon spreads his arms and spins. "Wow. It sure is heavy."

"You'll get used to it," Theo replies.

"I'm ready. Before I got so sick I couldn't do anything, I used to go to martial arts classes," Davon says. "Now that I'm better, I can't wait to do it again."

"I know all the martial arts," Theo says. "I would be proud to spar with you." He pats Davon on the shoulder. "Stay here." He ducks back into the trunk. When he emerges, he holds up a small vest, made of the same material as Davon's hauberk.

"Finn," he says. "This is for Riley. I converted it from the sleeves of the hauberk."

Theo tosses the mini-hauberk to me. It has slits in the back to put Riley's wings and four small holes for his legs. I help Riley step in, gently pull his wings through, and then I fasten the front across his chest. Riley tears across the clearing as if he has seen a squirrel.

Little show-off.

"We feel certain Riley will prove himself to be a valuable member of the team," Theo says, laughing. He bobs into the trunk again, and this time he pulls out a small bundle, snapping it to unfurl a yellow cloth smock. On the front is a coat-of-arms with some symbols and writing on it. I notice two familiar large slits in the back.

It occurs to me that the slits are for *Davon's wings.*

"This is to be worn over your hauberk whenever you wear it," Theo says. He points to the front. "This is the HALO coat-of-arms. You will learn more about that in another class." Davon pulls the smock over his hauberk. Theo stands back, beaming. "Congratulations, Davon. You are well on your way to discovering your place on the team."

Davon blushes. We give him a standing ovation. Nash rises last, clapping half-heartedly.

I wonder what's bothering him now, but I don't have time to worry about it. The gate to the back yard of the dormitory opens, and a soft, fragrant breeze blows across the clearing. The red-haired angel we saw the first night strides into view. I don't remember her being so tall; she's about six feet. Her hair curls to her shoulders, and she has the face of a movie star.

"I won't have any trouble paying attention to her," Karl whispers in my ear.

The angel carries a bag, which she drops at her feet. "You may call me Avicenne. I am your Instructor of Angel Health," she says.

I can't place her accent.

"I am responsible for teaching you how to understand and take care of yourself, other angels, and when necessary, human beings."

Avicenne tosses her hair, and it smells as if an entire field of exotic flowers has been stuffed up my nose. She picks up her bag, flicks her index finger, and we each hold a paperback book in our hands. It is titled *Angel Health: A Manual.* "Please read this before your lesson with me tomorrow," she says, laughing infectiously. The laugh sounds a little like machine gun fire. "There will be a quiz."

Everyone groans, except Mallory, who beams at Avicenne.

"Yes, Mallory. I know that you would appreciate that." Avicenne laughs again, closes the bag, and slings it over her shoulder. "See you all tomorrow. Happy reading."

Theo watches Avicenne all the way back to the gate, and when she's gone, he sighs.

Chapter 16
Angel Seminar

After our morning warfare class, we're back in Welcome Cottage for our second seminar.

Rouena's not there yet, and Nash wants us to play a joke on her by shielding into the furniture and jumping out to scare her when she arrives.

"You don't think she's going to find that funny, do you?" Mallory asks.

"As usual Mal-*function*, you miss the point," Nash responds.

"I'll do it," Davon says.

"Yeah, you shield, and I'll tell Rouena you've gone missing," Karl says.

"Whatever you have planned, you better do it fast," Valeria remarks. "Rouena is coming."

"Aw, forget it," Nash says. "I've got better things to do, anyway." He dives onto a couch and kicks off his flip flops.

Rouena wastes no time. "Sit everyone. I've been looking forward to our second meeting." She arranges herself on the bench, crossing one leg over the other. "This is your third day here," she says, "long enough for the shock to wear off. I'm sure you have comments or questions."

Only one. Last night, I had another dream. This one wasn't a nightmare, but I wonder if I want to bring it up.

Mallory, to no one's surprise, speaks first. "Rouena, I've been wondering what the sonnet at the door means."

"Hmmm," Rouena murmurs. "Do the rest of you have any ideas?"

I find it annoying when teachers tell you to ask questions, and then when you do, they make *you* answer them.

I look at Sofia. Of the two of us, she probably got a lot more out of that poem than I did. I expect her to give an opinion, but it's Nash who comments, surprising me again.

"It says we've been chosen, whether we like it or not," he says. "And it says we have to do things we don't want to do."

"Well, Nash," Rouena replies. "I'm sorry you found it so negative." She pauses. "But your point is well taken. You were brought here by our choice, not yours."

I remember something in the poem about saving men's souls," Karl says. "But how exactly will we do that?"

"Don't worry, Karl. It won't be the seven of you alone. All the angel communities work together."

"What's our part?" I ask.

"As fledglings, your tasks are to learn lessons and practice skills," Rouena says.

"I mean, what do the seven of us have to do to save souls?" I feel like she deliberately misunderstood my question.

"Actually, Finn, I am going to let someone else answer that," Rouena says. "Tonight. But I will tell you that each of you has a talent, and you will use those talents together. Once you realize what yours is, as some of you have already, you will be able to do much more than you thought possible."

Sofia sweeps a stray piece of hair from her eyes. "So, you're saying that my ability to paint is the reason I'm here?" she says.

"It's much more than that," Rouena answers.

"But what if I don't have a clue what my talent is?" Mallory says.

"Your talent is being annoying, Mal-*practice*," Nash says.

"Will you stop that?" Mallory yells. "Talk about being annoying."

"Oh, I could go on all day," Nash replies.

He reminds me of a cat batting at a cornered mouse.

"Ignore him," I hear Valeria whisper to Mallory. "You're giving him what he wants."

Mallory scuffs her foot back and forth on the floor and gives Nash what Garrett and I used to call *the stink eye*. She does it better than anyone I've ever seen. Garrett would have called her a professional.

"I found out this morning that I have a talent for warfare skills. I'm the best at shielding," Davon says. He still wears his hauberk and smock. "Theo says I'll use my bequest when we're fighting demons."

"Yes, Davon. I noticed your bequest. You look dashing, and you have found your niche," Rouena says.

"But wasn't that always your interest?" Mallory asks. "My interest is literature. What does that have to do with anything?"

I wonder briefly if my weird dreams have anything to do with my talent, but that seems dumb. I inventory my other abilities. Skateboarding? Singing?

"Rouena," Valeria says. "I'm interested in a lot of things. How will I know which one is my talent?"

"We're all here to help you with that," Rouena says, "Especially during this week's classes."

"I was also wondering something else. How come we're all about the same age? I mean, I'm fourteen. Everyone else is fourteen or fifteen, too. It seems to me that you would ask adults to help you instead of us."

"Yeah," Karl says. "I was wondering that, too. All this seems a huge responsibility for a bunch of teenagers."

"My point, ex-*actly*," Nash says.

Rouena threads her long, slender fingers together. "We were about your age when we came to HALO," she says, "young enough to be open to learning, but strong and mature enough to handle what would come our way."

"What *is* going to come our way?" Nash asks.

Sofia has been fidgeting for the past few minutes, not really listening. She interrupts the conversation, changing the subject. "Rouena," she says, "I really miss my parents. Will I be able to see them again?"

Sofia impresses me again with her ability to ask the question I want to ask but didn't think of. Dad is constantly on my mind. I worry about him. With both Mom and me gone, he must be devastated. A random thought strikes me, possibly the first that tells me I'm changing from human to angel. How would things have been different my last night on earth if I had known how to shield?

"You will all be able to watch over your family and friends on earth when you achieve the level of guardian, though they will not be able to see you. For now, you must stay on the grounds of HALO."

Nash hitches forward, his eyes burning. "Why?"

"As fledglings, you are vulnerable to demons," Rouena says. "You haven't got the skills to deal with them yet."

The room falls silent as we ponder that one.

After several uncomfortable moments, Rouena tells us our questions are excellent. "They show us you are ready."

"Ready for what?" Nash asks.

Rouena's expression is apologetic. She twists her necklace chain in her fingers. "I understand your impatience, Nash, I truly do. Tonight you will get some of the answers you seek. We are having a special meeting." She drops the necklace and uncrosses her legs. "How about ending our seminar for today? That will give you lots of time to go back to the dormitory and rest."

"Wait," Karl says. "Before we go, I've got a very, very important question. Ha, ha. I heard we will be eating a special meal at the meeting tonight. Is that true?"

"Yeah," Davon adds. "Avery told us."

"Avery is right," Rouena says. "It will be an

incredible meal."

Karl nods.

"Awesome," Davon says. He has lost the sickly pallor he had the first night. It's not hard to figure out he's happier here than he was on earth.

Everyone stirs, and I almost chicken out. "Um, maybe it's not the time, but something's been bothering me."

"What is it, Finn?" Rouena asks.

"The first night we were here, when we all told our stories, I noticed mine and Sofia's were different." I gaze at the ceiling. This is hard. "Most of you came here because of an accident, or, like Davon, from an illness. But, Sofia and I were murdered. Does that mean anything?"

I glance at Sofia. Valeria puts an arm around her.

Rouena and I lock eyes. I can tell she doesn't want to get into this, but when I don't look away, she answers. "We have been planning *The Thousand Year Change* for a long time. The plans included bringing you here and transitioning you from your human lives to your angel lives. When it came to you and Sofia, other forces reached you first."

"Yes," Sofia says, pulling up her knees and hugging them. "I can still feel that evil man's hands around my neck."

Snap. I recall the whole kidnapping—feel the repulsive slime and the startling pain and smell the vile odor of the creature. "Sofia, do you remember what happened to you after that—I mean, how you got here?" I ask.

"What do you mean, Finn?" Sofia tilts her face toward me.

If she doesn't remember anything else, anything like what happened to me, I'm not going to be the one to bring it up. "Nothing," I say. "I was wondering, that's all."

Valeria cuts in. "What about my family, Rouena? I'm the only one who lost my family as well. Have I lost them forever?"

"No one has lost anyone," Rouena says.

"That's crap," Nash says. "I don't see any of our families around here. How can you say we haven't lost anyone?"

"It's more complicated than that, Nash."

Nash smacks his forehead with his palm. "When is somebody going to give me a straight answer around here?"

I guess I better bring up the other topic. It's better than having Nash freak out. "Is anyone else having weird dreams?"

Rouena whips her head in my direction, her aqua eyes wide, but as she opens her mouth, Claude chugs through the door on his short bowed legs. He smiles at everyone. "Hello, fledglings. I hear all sorts of positive things about you so far. Yes, I certainly do hear good things." Claude reaches up to whisper something in Rouena's ear. She nods, smiles, and Claude scurries away.

"Lunch is waiting for you in the dormitory," Rouena says. "I will see you tonight in Council Cottage." She stands. "Finn, may I see you before you go?"

Shoot. What did I do?

After the others leave, Rouena puts her arm around my shoulder. "It seems that you have figured out that we almost lost Sofia and you," she says. She explains how demons got to us first and how the HALO angels scrambled to get us back. "It was touch and go there for a while."

I'm not sure I really understand what Rouena is saying, but I do know I don't want to think where I'd be if the angel with the sapphire-blue eyes hadn't saved me.

"You're here, Finn, and so is Sofia," Rouena says. "A crisis was averted. Let's leave it at that." She takes her arm away. "Now go. Something fun and very human is about to happen at the dormitory. Enjoy it."

When I get back, everyone is gathered around the kitchen island, feasting on sandwiches and drinking soda. Mallory makes me regret bringing up my question to Sofia about getting here.

"I don't remember anything funny about getting here, Finn," she says. "I mean, one second I saw the car, the next I felt the impact, but then I landed on that parking lot outside. Claude was there, standing at the door, watching. He pulled me right in. Did something happen after you got shot?"

"Nothing you need to worry about, Mallory."

"I woke up on Claude's couch," Valeria says. "I don't remember the trip either."

"Tell us about it, Finn," Nash says, laughing. "Did flying monkeys bring you here?"

"And what do you mean you're having weird dreams," Mallory says.

She can't let anything go, can she?

Luckily, I don't have to answer. Avery arrives, carrying a huge birthday cake. The multi-colored lighted candles chase each other around the top like lights on a movie theatre marquee, leaving streams of glimmer in the air.

"Hey, everyone. It's Karl's birthday," Avery announces. "I made his favorite, red velvet cake with vanilla cream cheese icing. It's time to celebrate."

"Yum," Karl says, smacking his lips.

"Hey, why didn't you say something, Karl?" Davon asks.

"And how can you have a birthday when you're dead, anyway?" Nash asks. He jabs Karl in the arm, but it's a playful jab.

Avery cuts us each a giant slice of cake, while Karl sits at the piano and plays *Happy Birthday*. It's a jazzy version, and when we start singing, I don't notice them dropping out. When the song is over, everyone is staring at me.

"Wow, you've got a set of pipes, Finn," Karl says, diving into a tune I know, an old Beatles song called *Here Comes the Sun*.

"Thanks," I say, and for the next hour, we pile more cake on our plates, hook elbows, cavort around the room, and sing at the top of our lungs. Even Nash joins in.

Chapter 17
A Lesson in Angel Health

Avicenne's class is located in the cottage nearest to the dorm. A message on her front board tells us to leave our manuals on the desks, go through the side door, and meet her next door in the Infirmary. Still high on sugar, we slip through an arched opening, and the first thing I see is Riley, lounging on one of the cots. He lifts his head and blinks.

"Hey, boy, you missed the party," I tell him, running my hands through his soft fur.

"Riley actually visits me quite often, Finn," Avicenne says. "He likes it here."

I give the place a quick once-over. It looks sort of like the nurses office at my middle school, and I think back to seventh and eighth grade, when after "the accident," I visited the nurse a lot. I always seemed to have a headache, a stomach ache, or both.

Nurse Pam would let me lie on the cot, where I

would close my eyes and listen to her hand out medications, make phone calls, or treat the other kids that came in. She never questioned me or called my dad, and after about half an hour, I'd feel better and go back to class. By the time I got out of middle school, I didn't get the headaches or stomach aches anymore.

Like Nurse Pam's office, posters line the Infirmary walls. They're freaky like the ones in Nurse Pam's, too. One is a cutaway of the organs in the human body, and another is titled *The Seven Chakras,* whatever they are.

The room is furnished with a long table in the middle, two cots against the wall, and lots of flowering plants. I realize one of the windows is the one I saw the other day on my bike ride with Nash. The same cat lies on the window sill, but the bird is perched on the shelf of a floor-to-ceiling cabinet.

Valeria walks to the cabinet, touching some of the glass jars filled with colorful materials. "I love this room," she says. "It's so comforting."

"Thank you, dear," Avicenne says. She pulls a rubber band off her wrist, and ties up her curls. With her long dress and funny shoes, I realize she reminds me of a sixties hippie chick, or at least what I've seen of them in pictures.

Avicenne tells us to gather around the table.

"Valeria has been talking nonstop about that health manual," Nash says.

"Yes. I have some questions," Valeria says.

Mallory picks up a large, ancient book from the table. She rifles through it. "I have some questions, too," she says.

"Of course, you do," Nash says. "But why don't you give someone else a chance?"

"I have plenty of answers for everyone," Avicenne says. "Can your questions wait, Valeria, or do you want to ask me something now?"

"May I?" Valeria asks.

Avicenne nods.

"Well, it seems like almost everything about our bodies is the same as when we were human. We still eat and sleep. So, could one of us break a bone or get a cold? I mean, is it possible that we might need to come here?"

Avicenne tells us we might, but most of the afflictions or illnesses that can plague a human can no longer affect us.

I think of Davon's remarkable improvement as she walks to the gigantic cabinet.

"I've been watching over you carefully since you arrived," Avicenne says. "You are moving away from the need for human care. In fact, if you needed me now, I would use methods doctors on earth do not."

"What do you mean?" Valeria asks.

Avicenne pulls two jars from the shelves. "I would use more holistic cures, such as the ones mentioned in your manual. Holistic means that you use the natural ingredients from nature to prevent or cure. But here, let me show you."

Setting the jars on the table, Avicenne grabs a mixing bowl from underneath. She opens one jar, pinches off a chunk of stinky green stuff, and throws it in the bowl. Then she scoops a cinnamon-like powder out of another jar, tossing that on top. The mixture begins to smoke. "Now, all I have to do is mix in the final ingredient." Opening a cabinet door, she takes a bottle of clear liquid from inside and pours a few drops into the bowl. The smoke dissipates, and the mixture solidifies.

Avicenne takes the block out of the bowl and sets it on the table. She flattens it with a pie dough roller and cuts it into bite-sized pieces.

"Are those for us?" Valeria asks.

Avicenne smiles. "It's something to help the digestion, sort of a food disintegration system. You see, you don't actually need food anymore, but we know it is a comfort to you. I've been putting this in your food at each meal."

"Wow," Valeria says. "I would love to learn about these things."

Mallory puts the book back on the table. "Avicenne, are we going to be taking that quiz on our homework reading?"

"Good job, Mal-*nutrition*," Nash says. "She might have forgotten about the quiz, but, no-o, you have to bring it up."

"There's no avoiding it, Nash," Avicenne says. She laughs like she did at warfare class, a contagious burst. "Okay, everyone back to the classroom. I'll give you five minutes to skim over the material one more time."

I like Avicenne. She's fun and easy on the eyes.

The quiz is a shocker. First, Avicenne gives us regular paper and pencil to take it, and second, Valeria, not Mallory, turns hers in first. Third, the moment Nash, who brings his up last, places his paper on the desk, Avicenne asks for our attention.

"I have graded the quizzes," she says.

"How the heck did she grade them already?" Nash asks. He's not even back to his seat.

"You have to remember where you are,"

Mallory says. "Anyway, I thought it was easy, didn't you?"

"Mal-*let*, you are a condescending nerd, and I can only hope—"

Avicenne's laugh shuts Nash down, and I realize that her laugh is like Claude's fan trick, a kind of tranquility booster. I make a mental note to try and figure out what the rest of the instructors are using on us.

Avicenne reaches into her desk drawer and pulls out a small leather bag with long straps. She rolls the bag back and forth in her hands.

"So, fledglings, about your grades. The highest quiz grade was earned by—drum roll, please." She nods to Karl, who *rat-a-tat-tats* on the desk until Avicenne pulls her fingers across the front of her neck and yells, "Cut."

Avicenne stands. "One of you is a young lady who shows a natural affinity for the subject of medicine. Can one of you perhaps guess who this is?"

"I know, I know," shouts Mallory.

"It's called a rhetorical question, Mal-*aise*," Nash says.

"My vote is Valeria," Karl says, strengthening my Karl-likes-Valeria theory.

"It *is* Valeria," Avicenne says, motioning for Valeria to come to the front of the room.

Valeria, blushing, walks to the front desk and stands beside Avicenne, who places the leather bag around Valeria's neck. "Valeria, you are the second of the fledglings to receive a bequest," Avicenne says. She does a few tap steps, laughs, and then hugs Valeria.

The door flies open, and Theo rushes in. "Have I missed the big reveal?" he asks.

112

"Not all. I'm getting ready to explain."

Theo leans against the blackboard, as Avicenne lifts the leather bag Valeria is wearing. "Inside this bag," she says, "is a bottle that contains a mixture of the most potent medicines used during our time on earth. The medicines are cures for ailments within each of the four temperaments. As you adjust to becoming angels in the next few weeks, this type of medicine will become more important to you."

Theo gestures for us to stand, and when he claps, we follow his lead. Karl puts his fingers in his mouth and blows a long loud wolf whistle.

"Yay, Valeria," Sofia shouts.

"Valeria and I will be spending a lot more time together, discussing all aspects of angel health," Avicenne says. "As for the rest of you, continue to use the manual as a reference. We will meet again next week. Class dismissed."

"Wait," Theo says. "Before they go, Avi, I want to share something with the fledglings."

"Theo, it's not necessary," Avicenne says.

"Yes, I believe it is," Theo says, extending his hand toward the leather bag around Valeria's neck. "Fledglings, this particular concoction was created by a remarkable woman who, a thousand years ago, was renowned throughout the world as an innovative and mystical healer."

"You mean Avicenne, don't you?" Valeria asks.

Avicenne's face turns almost as red as her hair.

"I only speak the truth, my dear," Theo says. He kisses Avicenne's cheek and congratulates Valeria. We all clap again as Valeria makes her way back to her seat. Karl gives her a high five.

I'm happy that another of us has found a place

within the group. Two down, five to go. I can't help but wonder when it will be my turn.

Chapter 18
The Story of Halo

Suits are laid out on our beds, and I get the message tonight is a special occasion. When we all meet together in the great room, the girls are jaw-dropping in their formal dresses.

The mood of excitement is contagious. Even Nash is not as sullen as usual. "You gonna walk with your girlfriend?" he teases.

"Funny," I reply. But, of course, I do walk with Sofia on the way to Council Cottage. She is gorgeous in her yellow strapless dress, and she smells fantastic.

The instructors are already there when we arrive, and they sit at a large, round wooden table.

"Wow, this is like King Arthur's Round Table," Mallory remarks. She goes off about Camelot as Avery shows the rest of us to our seats.

To my delight, I am seated next to Sofia. On my left, Theo sits beside Davon. Avicenne sits on the other side of Davon, then Valeria. Rouena is next to Valeria, and on Rouena's other side is Nash.

I can't believe someone had the dumb idea to put Mallory next to Nash, but she has her back to him anyway, engaged in a heated debate with Professor Guillaume. The wheelchair instructor is on the professor's other side, then Karl, then Sofia, and finally, the circle returns to me.

I hear snippets of conversation. Theo and Davon chat about how Davon's grandfather won a medal for bravery during some war. Karl and the wheelchair instructor are talking about Beethoven's Ninth Symphony. I think of Dad. Mallory and Professor Guillaume's debate is about whether Shakespeare actually wrote his plays. I relax, enjoy the scent of Sofia's hair, and let my eyes wander.

Out of the corner of my eye, I see something strange. I rub my eyes, and blink, but it's still there. I lean over to Sofia. "Hey, Sof, do the instructors look funny to you?" I whisper.

It comes to me. Honeysuckle. Her hair smells like honeysuckle.

"I was thinking the same thing. It's like they're blurry." She turns, and her face is inches from mine.

A surge of adrenalin almost knocks me out of my chair, and I have to lean back and catch my breath. A few seconds pass before I can talk again. "At first I thought it was because they are dressed up," I say, "but it's more like their outlines are smeared. And I see colors, too."

"We must be hallucinating," Sofia says, giggling.

Rouena taps her glass three times. The conversations stop. "I have good news and bad news," she says. It's one of my father's favorite sayings. "The

116

good news is, this your chance to dine on your favorite dishes."

We clap and cheer.

"What's the bad news?" Karl asks.

"The bad news is this is your last human meal."

Karl groans. "I was afraid you were going to say that."

"By the end of this evening, you will have shed the last of your human need for food."

"Sorry, man," I say to Karl, over Sofia's head.

The instructor in the wheelchair pats Karl on the arm. "You will not miss food, Karl," he says. "I promise there will be other distractions."

Mallory squeals as the table loads with platters full of cheeseburgers and fries, pizzas topped with everything I can think of, thick juicy steaks, fried chicken, and buttery corn-on-the-cob. Right in front of me, a mound of steaming mashed potatoes fills a huge bowl to the rim, and a plate of bacon wrapped scallops beckons. Glass pitchers of soda and tea are scattered among the food.

The instructors watch us as we devour plateful after plateful, laughing and talking with our mouths full.

I drench a French fry in gravy and grieve a little. I will miss this. Then I watch in wonder as my steak metamorphoses into bite-sized chunks. I stab one with my fork, dip it into the bloody juice, and cram it in my mouth.

While we eat, the room darkens. Candles appear, illuminating the room with flickering light. My steak disappears, but a dessert plate, loaded with peanut butter ice-cream, vanilla pudding, sugar cookies, and strawberry shortcake turns up in its place. I scarf down the sweets. Finally, Rouena announces the end of the feast, and everything on the table vanishes.

A soft breeze sweeps through the room, and the aroma is familiar to me, fresh cut wood. A woman materializes behind Valeria and Rouena. No compliments would ever do her justice. She shimmers. Blonde waves fall to her waist. She is accompanied by amazing choral singing, which continues for a few moments before it fades into peaceful silence.

The woman spreads her arms, and a pair of enormous wings, fanning out at least four feet on either side, cascade from her shoulders to the floor, each feather pristine white. Bright pink light surges from her body and pulses over us. A yellow circle glows above her head.

It's her sapphire-blue eyes that finally penetrate my dense brain. She is the one who caught me as I fell from the mouth of the monster. She is the angel who saved me.

Valeria breaks the reverent silence. She twists in her chair and gazes at the woman in awe. "All my life, this is how I pictured angels," she says.

Chairs scrape the floor as all but the instructor in the wheelchair stand and nod their heads in respect. The rest of us follow their example, until the magnificent angel motions for us to sit.

"Fledglings," Rouena says. "I would like you to meet Maddelena." The two women face each other, raise their palms, and a flash of light passes between them.

"Welcome to HALO School, fledglings," Maddelena says. She lifts her hands, and her wings ripple. "Sofia, Davon, Valeria, Nash, Mallory, Karl." She nods and smiles at me. Other than Sofia's smile, hers is the most dazzling I've ever seen. "Finn," she says. "Nice to see you, again."

I nod back, dumbstruck. Maddelena doesn't actually speak. Instead, I'm *hearing* her thoughts.

"Your arrival is a momentous occasion for us," she says. "And I am here tonight to tell you the tale of the creation of HALO."

Maddelena's disembodied voice spills over us like echoing chimes. She hovers about a foot above the floor, and her entire being emits serenity vibes.

"Long ago, earth existed in two equal parts. One side was light and the other side was dark. The spirits who lived in the light were very different from those in the dark, and they managed to coexist by staying away from each other."

Like Professor Guillaume's demonstration with the stone.

"After many years," Maddelena continues, "the light had an unusual effect on the earth's surface. It caused growth. Earth began to sustain life, and creatures called humans eventually evolved. The spirits on the light side fell in love with the innocence and simplicity of their accidental creations, but the spirits on the dark side hated them."

I wonder what the humans could have done to make the dark spirits hate them.

Maddelena retracts her wings with a snap and floats to the floor. "The Light Spirits helped their creatures by giving gifts, like fire and tools."

I visualize cave men wearing animal skins, rubbing sticks together to build a fire, and chasing animals with spears.

"They taught humans to respect and love one another, and when it was time for the humans to leave their earthly bodies behind, they even allowed human souls to go to the same reward where the Light Spirits went."

Professor Guillaume clears his throat. The sound echoes.

"Many centuries passed. Humans accomplished great things. But soon it became apparent that the Dark Spirits had found ways to tamper with them. The Dark Spirits influenced some humans to behave badly, even to kill each other. The Light Spirits became terrified as they realized they were now competing with the Dark Spirits for the souls of their beloved creations."

Maddelena circles the table behind us. She stops and places her hands on Sofia's shoulders. Pink light seeps into Sofia's body, and Sofia visibly relaxes, smiling contentedly. "To try to save humanity, the Light Spirits formed a coalition of communities. Each community had a job which would help protect human souls from the influence of the Dark Spirits, and each Light Spirit was allowed to volunteer to become a member of a community. The volunteers were called angels."

Maddelena lifts her hands from Sofia's shoulders. "For a time, all was well," she says. "The various angel communities were able to save humanity from extinction."

She steps sideways and touches me. What I feel is indescribable. "Then, about a thousand years ago, a problem arose, one that threatened humanity once again. The Dark Spirits found a new weapon, which they called the demon, a human soul that the Dark Spirits had been able to steal, infuse with evil, and send back to earth again. This weapon could walk among its peers on earth and influence them to choose the path of evil."

Maddelena lifts her hands from my shoulders, moving past Theo to Davon. "Demons were able to steal hundreds more souls than the Dark Spirits could reach by themselves, and both the Light Spirits and the angel communities feared for humanity once again. For you see, neither the Light Spirits nor the angels were able to recognize the difference between a demon and a regular human being."

She pauses. "Unbelievably, a miracle occurred. Angels discovered a few humans on earth who had the ability to identify demons among their fellow man. Of course, these humans were approached and asked for their help."

Maddelena releases her wings. They shoot out like powerful white waves, and the force pushes me back in my seat like the g's of a rocket takeoff. "Rouena, Theo, Guillaume, Avicenne, Lionel, Sweyn, and I were those humans. We were brought from earth, the first humans to become angels, and here we formed the HALO community."

Sofia nudges my arm and nods in the direction of Theo and Professor Guillaume. The two instructors as we knew them are gone. Instead, each has a wavering colorful outline, a set of full-length wings, and a yellow halo. I look around to see that the other instructors have changed as well.

Maddelena sweeps her graceful hand in the air. "Since forming HALO ten centuries ago, the seven of us have worked with the other angel communities, and humanity has continued to flourish."

Maddelena rises, fanning the air with her wings, and once again I breathe fresh cut wood.

"And so I come to the end of my tale. For you see, soon it will be time for us, the first HALO team, to go to our reward, the Light. It is *The Thousand Year Change* we were promised by the Light Spirits."

My heart begins to pound. I know what's coming.

Maddelena speaks the words that change everything. "You are the human descendants we have brought here to replace us. *You are the next HALO team.*"

Chapter 19
A Bit of Worry

After Maddelena leaves, we burst into excited chatter. The instructors watch, and after a few moments, Rouena quiets us. Her outline is beautiful, aqua blue like her eyes. "It's time for the seven of you go back to the dormitory to absorb what you have just heard and seen."

Mallory raises her hand. Rouena sighs.

"I will answer one question, Mallory," Rouena says.

"What did she mean—we're your descendants?" she asks.

"That is one for our next seminar. You have enough to digest for the moment."

Mallory continues to wave her hand. "You didn't answer that one, so can I ask another?" she asks.

Rouena laughs. "Okay, you got me."

"I understand the wings and halos, but what are

all the outline colors?"

"Those are our auras," Rouena says. "All angels have them. They represent our energy and our personalities. Different colors mean different things. My aura is mainly blue, which means a balanced existence is important to me. Green, for example, means that angel has a natural healing force."

We all look at Avicenne, whose aura is green.

"We have things to attend to," Rouena says, "and you must go rest. You can imagine you will need all your strength for the next few weeks."

I feel Sofia's hand grab for mine. She squeezes it. I squeeze back.

We stagger back to the dormitory. Riley curls at my feet, and I see everyone settle in to listen to Karl play piano, except Nash, who has disappeared. I let the music calm me and take me to another place. I imagine I am dancing with Sofia. Her head rests on my chest and her arms drape around my shoulders.

"So they got to choose to come here," Nash says, jerking me back to reality. He has reappeared, and he's slouching against the pinball machine, breathing hard.

Something in the tone of his voice makes us all give him our full attention. Karl stops playing.

"Well, I didn't. They think they can just pluck us off the face of the earth and bring us here because it's been a thousand years or something?" Nash's voice rises. "What's up with that?" He steps away from the pinball machine. "And they're crazy if they think I know what a demon looks like. I'm a fifteen year old *kid*."

"But you must have the ability to recognize them," Valeria says. "We all must have it." She stands, but she doesn't try to walk toward Nash or touch him.

"Yeah, if we are their descendants, we must have inherited whatever it is they can do, right?" I say, more to myself than to Nash. My words are falling on deaf ears anyway. Nash crosses his arms tight across his chest, and his face is beet red.

"I choose to be here," Davon says.

"Yeah, well you believe in aliens, too," Nash says, scornfully.

"I choose to be here, too," I say. "How about you, Karl?" I hope if we all agree, Nash will calm down.

"Yeah, I want to help," Karl says. "I'm okay with it here. I hardly miss my human life at all anymore."

"Me neither," Mallory says. "I'm in."

"I'll do whatever they need me to do," Sofia says.

"Nash," Valeria says. She takes a small step toward him. "It sounds like what we're going to do here is important. More important than our lives on earth."

"*One for all and all for one,*" Mallory quotes.

Hasn't she learned by now not to do stuff like that?

"You people are acting like a bunch of brainwashed idiots," Nash says, turning away from us. "I'm out of here." He stomps down the hallway.

After he's gone, Valeria walks to the entrance of the hallway, listening for a moment. "Do you think he'll be all right?" she asks. "I'm worried about him."

"I'm sure he'll come around," I say, not sure at all.

"If he knew what his talent was, he might feel better," Karl says. "Maybe it would help him forget about his girlfriend."

"Yeah, I'd like to know what mine is, too," I say. "I've kind of narrowed it down to singing, but what would I sing?

For some reason, a song Garrett's older brother Sean wrote for his band, Fools and Horses, comes to mind, and I make up a little ditty to its tune right on the spot. I use Riley's rubber bone as a makeshift microphone.

> *"At HALO we got mad skill,*
> *So demons find you, we will,*
> *From us you can never hide,*
> *We'll search for you far and wide."*

When everyone laughs, I know I have my audience, and I really dig in. "And here's the chorus."

> *"We will see you,*
> *We will find you,*
> *You are evil,*
> *And we have a job to do."*

More laughs and a round of applause.

"You know, Finn, maybe none of our talents have anything to do with identifying demons," Sofia says, still giggling. "I get the impression it's something completely different, something we can all do."

Sofia has a good point. She's beautiful *and* smart.

Mallory pipes up. "What I'd like to know is who are Lionel and Sweyn?"

"Lionel is the Demonology instructor," Karl says. "I sat next to him at dinner."

"Well then, have any of you seen Sweyn?

Mallory asks. "He hasn't been here. Including Maddelena, we've only seen six of them, you know."

"Sweyn? Where did you hear that name?" Davon asks.

"Maddelena said he was one of them, too," Mallory says.

Davon's eyebrows lift. "Oh, I must have missed that. There was so much going on."

"Right," I say, realizing for the first time how exhausted I am. And I guess I should probably try to talk to Nash, after all, he is my roommate. "I think I'll go to bed," I say, reluctant as always to leave Sofia.

When I open the door to our room, Nash is turned toward the wall. I figure any conversation will have to wait until morning.

I fall into bed. My mind races, but sleep comes quickly. To my relief, I don't dream.

Kip Taylor

Day 4

There are some things you learn best in calm and some in storm.

-Willa Cather

Kip Taylor

Chapter 20
A Lesson in Angel History

I'm the last one awake, and when I get to the great room, breakfast is conspicuously absent. Karl looks depressed. I drop next to Sofia and listen in on the conversation.

Claude has dropped by for a visit. He's almost lost in the cushions of the couch, but he looks the same, except I can see his aura peeking out from underneath his shirt. It's a light shade of orange, not as intense as any of the instructors'. "The HALO angels were preparing for you, but they had their original jobs to do as well," he says. "We were brought here in the middle of the twentieth century in anticipation of your arrival. We were to help with the transition of teams. It is a great honor, of course, and it was right after—"

"I came a few years later," Avery says, stepping around the corner from the entrance foyer and cutting Claude off mid-sentence. He's wearing the most outlandish outfit yet, a Disco Era metallic suit with flared pants and silver platform shoes. "Before us, HALO had no assistants. Some of the other communities had them. We only stay for a hundred years, you see, not a thousand."

I try to find Avery's aura, but the metallic material sort of blinds me, so I quit looking. Instead, I check for Nash. I don't see him anywhere. He must be avoiding us.

"So far, most of the plans have gone smoothly," Claude says, "and it seems your education is well on its way." He grins.

Most of the plans?

Avery tilts his head a moment and cups his hand behind his ear. "The professor is ready for you," he says.

"Shouldn't we wait for Nash?" Mallory asks.

I can't believe that came out of her mouth.

"He's probably already waiting for you at Past House," Claude says. "He came to visit me earlier. Independent, isn't he?"

"That's one word for him," Mallory replies.

Avery and Claude wave goodbye after we traipse over to Past House, where Professor Guillaume waits at the front door. His halo, wings, and aura are gone.

"Where are—" Mallory begins.

"Before you arrived, we instructors made a decision to teach in our human form," Professor Guillaume says. "We hoped this way you would pay more attention to our lessons."

"I think you are right," Sofia says, smiling. "I would be thinking about how I would paint you."

I look for Nash again, but he's not here, either.

This makes me uneasy, though I'm not quite sure why. I bet Nash, aka Mr. Distractible, was the first consideration when the instructors made the decision to stay in human form.

"As soon as Nash gets here, we're going on a field trip," the professor announces. "You can't go to modern-day earth until you get your wings, but I can take you back in time for a history lesson. I want to show you a town that is very important to HALO, and while we're there, I will show you some art."

"Art," Sofia says. "What kind of art?"

"Angel art, in its original form," Professor Guillaume replies. "I thought you might be excited about that, Sofia. You will see how angels first appeared to humanity."

"Do angels look different today?" Mallory asks.

"They can. Especially during the time of HALO's existence, we have had to strategize. Demons are constantly improving their tactics. Sometimes we have shown ourselves, and sometimes we have had to back away."

"I'm in favor of backing away." It's Nash, striding in the back door.

"Ah, just in time, Mr. Anthony. Let's get underway."

The professor approaches one of the walls covered in paintings. He leans forward, tucks his thumb up under his fingers, and motions clockwise. A large hole opens up in the wall. "This is called a portal. Portals are the way we watch over humanity from our communities."

It's the same kind of hole I saw in my dream.

"Couldn't you just use Facebook or Skype?" Nash asks.

"Very funny, young man," Professor Guillaume says. "Our teaching techniques may seem old-fashioned to you, but what we have to teach you hasn't changed for centuries." He forms us into a line. "Follow me. One at a time, please."

It's actually a tunnel, and we have to crouch a little once we're inside, but like peering through a telescope, I can see the light at the other end. We emerge on a street between two rows of cottages. A high stone wall runs behind them, casting shadows on the cobblestones.

Men in tunics and tights cluster in small groups, chatting. Women in long skirts and head scarves, carrying buckets, stroll to and from a large round well in the middle of the street. I inhale a strange musky mix of roasting meat and horse manure.

"We modeled HALO after Wyattholme," the professor says, "a small town in England, where Maddelena and her family lived during the eleventh century." He motions to us. "This way."

"Can they see us?" Davon asks.

I hope not. We'd be like aliens with our jeans and t-shirts.

"We are invisible," Professor Guillaume says. "This is a day like any other to them."

We pass near the well, where a man and woman stand behind a cart, selling eggs and vegetables. Their horse is tied to a post on the narrow side street behind them.

"Maddelena's father owned this town, as well as all the land outside these walls," Professor Guillaume tells us. "The peasants worked for him in return for protection, and the King taxed any profit. The King's soldiers were brutal, and everyone was subject to their

134

terrorism."

As we continue walking, the professor lectures us in medieval angel history. "Has anyone heard of Joan of Arc?" he asks.

Mallory raises her hand. "I have," she says. "I read about her in a book. When she was thirteen, she heard a voice and saw light. She believed it was an angel, telling her to lead the French army against the English. They burned her at the stake for being a witch."

Professor Guillaume purses his lips. "Very good, but you left out one thing, Mallory. Joan of Arc was later made a saint."

"Really? Wow," Mallory comments.

"You mean there's something you don't know?" Nash asks in a snide voice.

"Ha, ha." Mallory shoots Nash *the stink eye* again.

"But since you bring up the subject of witchcraft," the professor says, "I'll tell you a little known fact about Shakespeare."

"Her hero," Nash says.

"Shakespeare modeled Prospero, the magician in *The Tempest*, after a man name Dr. Dee, a man who talked with angels through a human name Edward Kelley."

"How fascinating," Nash says.

"Nash," Valeria whispers. "Stop it." She bumps into him gently with her hip.

"Unfortunately, people began to fear Mr. Kelley," the professor says.

"You mean they thought it was black magic?" Mallory asks.

"Yes, but it was demons' work, of course."

I swear these two could talk twenty-four-seven.

"People always fear what they do not understand," Professor Guillaume continues.

"People fear boredom, too," Nash quips.

The professor has finally had enough. "Is that so? Well, young man, I hope we won't be boring you too much longer." We pause in front of one of the cottages, where the professor taps on the door. To my surprise, it is opened by Rouena. "Rouena," Professor Guillaume says, surprised. "Where is Maddelena?"

"She has been called away." Rouena steps into the sunshine, dressed in the same attire as the rest of the female townspeople.

"Happy to have you, then. We're headed to the church."

We continue up the street, turning the corner and arriving at our destination. Rouena climbs the steps to the carved wooden double doors. Though much smaller, the doors are similar to the ones at the entrance to HALO. A small tapestry hangs from a nail midway up the right door.

"Please, gather around," Rouena says. She faces us, putting one hand under the tapestry cloth and pointing to it with the other. "Back in our day, a family's coat-of-arms was carefully selected to represent what they stood for. This was the coat-of-arms of the Wyatts, Maddelena's family."

"Hey, that's almost the same as the one on my smock," Davon says. "Cool."

"That's correct, Davon. Would you like to know what the symbols mean?"

"I'd like that, too," Mallory says.

The rest of us nod.

Rouena points out each part of the shield. "The

136

horseshoe represents safeguard against evil, the flag, reward for valiant service, and the tree, the mystical connection between heaven and earth. The message on the banner, *Decoris ac Benefacti*, means dignity and service in Latin, the language of our time." She drops her hand and turns to face us again. "What you do not see here is the symbol we added to represent the HALO community, angel's wings for glory and honor wrapped around the shield."

We enter the church, murmuring to each other about our favorite parts of the coat-of-arms. At first, it's dark and musty, but as the professor latches the door open, the sun shines on the rich brown of the wooden pews. As we walk the length of the aisle toward the altar, the light changes, filtering through the colors in the stained glass and giving the altar and the front pews the look of a child's finger-painting.

"We must be quiet here," Professor Guillaume whispers. "This is a sanctuary."

"The stained glass is incredible," Sofia says under her breath.

"I love that one," I say, pointing to a farm scene, complete with sheep, dogs, and a field of grain.

Professor Guillaume arranges us in a semi-circle at the altar. The floor in front is marked with names and dates.

"What are these?" Nash asks.

"Those are grave markers," Mallory says.

"Remember to keep your voices down, please," the professor says.

"You mean people are buried under the church floor?" Valeria asks in a shocked whisper.

"To be buried inside the church was an honor," Professor Guillaume says. He points to the ceiling. "But here is what I brought you to see."

We lift our eyes. Through the rafters, pink-cheeked angels, dressed in long white robes, wings spread and halos glowing, fill the cloudy blue sky of the painted ceiling.

"Notice how the angels were rendered by the artist, who was allowed to see us as we truly are," the professor says.

"But, what about their auras?" Mallory asks, her voice echoing a little. "They aren't in the painting."

"Sheesh, Mal-*adjustment*," Nash whispers. "Could you be any louder?"

"The less a demon knows about an angel, the better," says the professor. "That's why their auras are covered with robes. And see that group on the right?"

"You mean the group that's singing?" I ask.

"Oh boy, I can't wait to put on my robes and go caroling," Nash says.

I stifle my laughter as much as I can.

The professor lowers his eyes. He plucks his pipe from his pocket and points it at Nash. "Young man, someday you may find that you will want to sing. It's a joyous form of communication. Isn't that right, Finn?"

"He was sure singing the other day at Karl's birthday party," I say, "even if he did search everywhere for the tune." I tap Nash's arm lightly. "Just kidding, my man."

I'm enjoying this field trip, and I've even figured out Professor Guillaume's pipe is the way he calms us, even if it doesn't seem to be working very well on Nash. If this class was on earth, no doubt the professor would be giving Nash the boot.

But Professor Guillaume has moved on. He's

asking Karl a question about the musical instruments in the painting, when suddenly loud, frantic screams erupt outside. A woman tears through the open doors, tripping over her skirts and throwing herself between two pews. She flops on the floor with a loud thud and I hear her moaning. Two soldiers dressed in hauberks and helmets ride up outside, waving their swords in the air and shouting in some unintelligible language.

"Oh, dear," Professor Guillaume says. "I'm afraid we are about to see more than we bargained for. Rouena, we must abort our visit quickly and return to HALO."

Rouena, her glance traveling between us and the doors, quickly opens a portal. "Ladies first," she says, ushering Valeria, Mallory, and Sofia toward the gap.

Mallory resists, crossing over to the professor and grabbing him by the arm. "Why are they chasing after that woman?" Professor Guillaume takes a step back, sizing up the soldiers as they dismount. "We have to stop this," Mallory says.

"We can't, Mallory," Rouena says in a solemn voice. "This happened almost a thousand years ago. Whatever happened to her then cannot be changed. We must let it happen."

The soldiers clamor up the steps toward the doors.

"They're going to kill her," Mallory wails. "We can't stand here and do nothing."

"Stand back, Mallory," Professor Guillaume says, pushing Mallory behind him and spreading his arms to shield her. *"Blow, blow, thou winter wind!"* he shouts. His words echo off the stone walls. The doors slam shut.

"How did you do that?" Mallory asks, gaping.

"My apologies, Rouena," the professor says, ignoring Mallory. "That was irresponsible and impulsive of me."

"I understand," Rouena replies. "You could not help yourself."

Outside, the soldiers shout and bang against the doors. The peasant woman crawls out from between the pews on her hands and knees. She stares at the door, then at the altar, her face tear-stained, her jaw slack.

"She can see us now, can't she," Sofia says.

"Yes," Rouena says. "The professor has interfered with history."

Professor Guillaume closes the remaining space between himself and the peasant woman. He helps her to her feet and ushers her through the door at the back of the altar.

The front doors burst open the moment they vanish. The soldiers stand for a moment, their eyes adjusting to the darkness.

"Professor Guillaume saved her," Mallory says, as Rouena reaches her and pulls her over to the portal by the arm.

"Yes, Mallory, he did. And now we must save ourselves."

Rouena shoves Valeria, Sofia, and Mallory through the portal. Karl steps through right behind, followed by Davon. "Nash, your turn. Go!" Rouena cries.

I back toward the portal, but I stop when I see the professor, wings spread, swoop down from the rafters. He hovers over the soldiers, as Rouena wraps her hands around my waist and throws me into the portal. The last thing I see is one of the soldiers, his

140

sword raised, his expression surprised.

Then I'm back in Past House. Rouena spills out of the portal opening, and a few seconds later, a ball of feathers spills out behind her. The feathers land in a pile, the portal shuts with a loud crack, and Rouena yells, "I'll take care of it, Guillaume," before she disappears.

The pile of feathers stands, shakes, and from the dust and dander, Professor Guillaume appears. He contracts his wings. "Please take your seats," he says.

"Obviously," he says, brushing himself off, "that was not planned. But these things happened in our time. Peasants were often killed by the King's soldiers."

"Why?" Davon asks.

"Various reasons," the professor answers. "None of them very good ones."

"Where did you take that poor woman?" Mallory asks.

"To a place of safety," Professor Guillaume says. He shakes his head, and his halo and aura disappear. Once again he stands before us, as if nothing happened, looking every inch the college professor, with his tweed suit and his magical pipe peeking out from its jacket pocket.

When we stand to go, the professor clears his throat. "Believe it or not," he says, "class is not over."

We sit back down, and the professor reaches under his desk, pulling out a flat leather briefcase. "Mallory, will you please come up here?"

Mallory pushes up her glasses. "Me?" she asks, pointing to herself. She stands and strides, head high, shoulders back, with a huge smile on her face, to the front of the room.

"You inspired me today, Mallory," Professor Guillaume says. "You reminded me what we're here for. Because you were so adamant, I felt as if I had to take the risk to change something in history. So I did, and we saved a woman's soul today."

"You mean those soldiers were demons?" Mallory asks. "And why was it a risk to save her?"

The professor nods. "Changing history is always a risk. There is a thing called The Domino Effect. And for ourselves, once we have been seen as angels, demons can trace our whereabouts and find us."

"But it was worth it, right?"

"Yes, Mallory. I believe it was."

I feel a familiar jolt and realize Rouena left to tell Claude we had to move once again.

Meanwhile Professor Guillaume unwinds the strap of the briefcase. "Soon enough," he says to all of us, "you will not have your instructors around to assist you. It is important to make sure all of you have your bequests. Mine is for Mallory."

He removes a thick book, yellowed with age, and holds it so that everyone can see the cover. I start to make out the letter "B," when Mallory jumps up, knocking over a chair. "That's not a copy of *Beowulf*, is it?" she screams.

"A copy?" Professor Guillaume says. "No." He holds it out to Mallory. "It is, however, the original manuscript."

"Somebody catch me. I'm going to faint. How did you get it?"

The professor clears his throat and casts his eyes to the floor. "Well, Mallory, my dear," he says. "A long, long time ago, I wrote it."

"You are the anonymous author of *Beowulf*, the

most important epic poem of the Middle Ages?"
Mallory screeches.

Professor Guillaume bows his head. "I am," he
says.

Mallory puts her hand out to shake his, pulls it
back, and throws herself into his arms, kissing him
several times on the cheek. "I'm gob smacked!" she
says. "I don't know what to say."

"That'll be the day," Nash says.

The professor's head bobs up and down, and
through the edges of his tweed jacket a bit of his
midnight blue aura peeks through.

"I can't wait to read it," Mallory squeals,
clutching the manuscript to her chest with both hands.

"And you must," Professor Guillaume says. "In
fact, it's very important that you do."

"Does it have something to do with my talent,
like Davon's and Valeria's bequests?" Mallory asks.

"I can't give you all the answers, my dear. There
are some things you must do all on your own." The
professor smiles. "And now, everyone, Lionel is
waiting. I must not encroach upon his time. His
classroom is across the bridge behind Past House. Use
the back door." Chairs scrape the floor, and we head
out.

Lionel is the instructor in the wheelchair. I'm
not looking forward to his class; the one Karl has told
us is called Demonology.

Chapter 21
A Lesson in Demonology

Lionel's domain is a small castle built of gray stone, hidden behind a forest. To get there, we walk down a sloping path and across a bridge that curves over a wide rushing stream. Riley joins us as we get to the bridge.

"This is a moat," Mallory says. "All authentic castles have them."

"Your wealth of knowledge is a constant source of wonder, you know that?" Nash says, turning to me and miming Mallory's way of pushing up her glasses and scrunching her nose. He almost runs into Davon, who has stopped to peer over the side of the bridge.

I watch Riley plow through the stream, using his wings to lift him when it gets deep.

"Next time, I'm going to try the water, too," Davon says.

"I don't know if that's such a good idea," Sofia

says. "It seems pretty treacherous."

"I could jump from rock to rock," Davon says. "It would be fun."

This is not the first time Davon has reminded me of a little kid. "It might be fun," I say.

Riley emerges on the other side of the stream, his white fur streaked with mud. He shakes.

"Lionel needs the bridge for his wheelchair, though, doesn't he," Valeria says.

"Speaking of Lionel, there he is," Karl says.

I follow his gaze a few yards down the path. Lionel sits at the castle door. He greets each of us with an enthusiastic handshake as we enter the castle.

Inside, the room is damp, musty, and cave-like. If there are any windows, they are covered. I'm claustrophobic to begin with, and in here I'm hot and sick to my stomach. I feel like we're cattle being led to slaughter, and after the incident this morning in the church, I'm not sure I'm ready to deal with this.

A large tapestry depicting a fierce battle looms behind the front lectern, and I feel even worse when my mind starts to play tricks on me. I think I hear the horses from the tapestry neigh and the swords clash. I also notice a man in the center of the tapestry, with a wooden object propped against his blood-soaked body. I'm pretty sure he's dead, and the thought makes me feel faint.

I gaze around the room to avoid looking at the tapestry, but others depicting similar scenes hang on the rest of the walls. Each is as bloody and repulsive as the original one. I can't get away from the violence.

I force my eyes back to our instructor, who has rolled his chair to the front of the room. "I'm Lionel," he says, in a booming voice. "But I'm sure Karl has already told you."

Lionel is dressed in a brown linen robe, tied with a rope. "I am the liaison between HALO and the rest of the angel communities. From me, you will learn about our enemies." He pauses. "Demons."

The way he says the word makes my stomach churn again. In a flash of empathy, I wonder if Nash has felt sick like this all along.

"I have my reasons for the darkness as well as for having nothing but the tapestries on display," he says. "Most of my belongings are extremely dangerous. In fact, I must implore you to keep your hands away from the tapestries at all times."

Bizarre thoughts creep into my brain. How can an angel be in a wheelchair? Was Lionel injured by demons? Why can't Avicenne cure him? I blink, overwhelmed, and then I notice the look on Sofia's face, and I forget about everything else. "Sofia," I whisper. "Are you okay?"

She nods. "Just a little bit nervous," she whispers. "This place scares me."

"I'm a little nervous, too," I admit. Who am I kidding—I can hardly breathe.

"I spent the last few years during my time on earth as a member of a religious order," Lionel says. "I brought these tapestries with me from the monastery, as well as a library of exquisite hand written manuscripts. Many are devoted to the study of demons and demonology."

Mallory raises her hand. "Excuse me, Lionel; are we going to be able to read some of the manuscripts? Can we sign them out?"

I wait for a remark from Nash, but he is quiet.

"The books are available to all of you.

However, you will not be able to sign them out, nor would you want to. They are far too large and cumbersome for you to carry."

Mallory nods and sits back.

I use my sleeve to wipe the sweat off my brow as I wonder if I will ever want to read one of Lionel's books.

"Maddelena has told you about your jobs, has she not?" Lionel continues. "You will be identifying demons for all the angel communities. To do so, you will need to know as much about your enemy as possible." He runs his hands over the wheels of his chair, and it moves a few inches closer to us. His voice lowers, and we strain to hear him. "They walk among humans without being recognized for the evil they are. Without HALO angels, humanity would be doomed."

I recall Guillaume's first history class again, the one where we got him off topic. Somehow the idea of demons wasn't so bad then. But here, in this room, I can't find a position in my chair where my body doesn't feel uncomfortable. I glance at the rest of the group. Everyone seems ill-at-ease.

"You mean they can look like anyone?" Mallory asks.

I imagine Nash saying, *Yes, Mallory, especially like you.* But Nash seems to be barely listening. He's slumped down in his seat, his breathing shallow and his face pale.

"Precisely," Lionel says. "Humans have no way of distinguishing demons from any other human beings. When demons possess human bodies, they are capable of exploiting human weaknesses, such as the desire for wealth and privileges or fear of pain."

Lionel flicks his finger, and a scroll, tied with

147

twine, appears on each of our desks.

I can't wait until they teach us the finger flick skill.

"Go ahead and unroll your copies, please. We will read together, so if you have any questions, we can address them immediately."

I gaze at the list, an outline written in elegant calligraphy, which reminds me of the sign-in register.

Lionel reads the title. "The Demon Arsenal."

Valeria raises her hand. "What is an arsenal?"

"It's a collection of weapons," Mallory says.

I wait, but again, no comment comes from Nash. What's the matter with him?

"Valeria, why don't you continue reading for us?" Lionel asks.

"Sure," Valeria says. "Part I. How Demons Manifest Themselves: #1. Shape-shifters."

"Only a very few demons are talented enough to be shape-shifters," Lionel says. "One is Foelle, the partner of Jarray. He is the general of the most fearsome demon army, The Righteous. Those two demons are a powerful couple, and I can only hope you never have to meet them face to face."

Shuddering, I flash back to the monster that seized me right after I was killed. "I think I may have met a shape-shifter," I say.

"What do you mean, Finn?" Sofia asks.

Everyone looks at me, and I swallow hard. "I was intercepted by a shape-shifter on my way here, I think," I say. "I mostly remember that it stank, and it had really sharp teeth."

"That's nasty," Davon says.

"It burned the skin right off my bones," I say.

"Why didn't you tell us this before?" Sofia asks.

"Yeah," Nash says, sitting up straight. "That might be something I'd want to know."

"I don't know," I say. "But I wouldn't be here if it wasn't for Maddelena. She saved me."

"You already knew Maddelena?" Valeria asks wide-eyed.

Apparently, I'm disappointing everyone.

"Just be glad he did," Lionel says. "Now, will someone else please read?"

Mallory raises her hand, but Lionel calls on Karl. "Keep reading until I tell you to stop," Lionel says.

"#2. Rats and other vermin, #3. Spiders, snakes, and various insects, #4. Ordinary humans."

"And which of those do you think is the most dangerous?" Lionel asks.

Sofia, Mallory and I raise our hands.

"Sofia?"

"Snakes, definitely snakes," Sofia says.

I grin.

"Finn?"

"Easy. Shape-shifters."

"Mallory?"

"Ordinary humans."

"Correct, Mallory," Lionel says.

Mallory tosses her hair and clears her throat. *"Be not afraid of greatness: some are born great, some achieve greatness, and some have greatness thrust upon 'em.'"* She smiles.

Nash turns to me and says, loud enough for everyone to hear, "I'd like to thrust the back of my hand across her self-satisfied face."

Finally, Nash is back to himself. I want to laugh, but I feel like we're not supposed to laugh in here.

"Prove my point, Nash," Mallory says.

"And why, do you suppose," Lionel says, "the most dangerous demons are those who appear as ordinary humans?"

Everyone is silent. I ponder all the people I knew in my lifetime and wonder which ones could have been demons. Mrs. Wolford, my middle school principal, comes to mind. I raise my hand.

"Finn?"

"Because you wouldn't necessarily know that a person was a demon," I say. "You might trust the person and have your guard down."

"So how do we recognize them?" Sofia blurts.

"Ah," Lionel answers. "You are beginning to see why your job as HALO angels is so important."

"But you didn't answer—" Mallory says.

"It would be irresponsible for me to give you all the answers," Lionel says, sounding like Professor Guillaume. "Some you must discover for yourselves." He raises an eyebrow. "Now, where were we? Finn, will you read Part II.?"

I pick up my scroll. "Part II. How Demons Instill Fear in Humans: #1. Natural disasters, #2. Accidents, #3.Abuse: (i.e. drug, alcohol, physical), #4. Murder, #5. Acts of Violence: (i.e. terrorism, war)."

"Thank you, Finn." Lionel takes a deep breath. "And so, I believe you are ready for a bit of hands-on experience." He grins. "A little test, if you will."

"Uh, oh," Karl says. "I hope this isn't another field trip."

Lionel pivots his wheelchair and reaches for the hanging tapestry behind him, the one that has been staring down at us the whole time. With both hands, he jerks it from the wall, spins his wheelchair back around, and throws it. The tapestry falls like dead leaves from a tree, settling over us.

I'm plunged into darkness.

I topple to the floor, and the dust from the old wool clogs my nose and throat and scratches my eyes. I choke and cough. I hear Sofia scream. Karl laughs, but it is a high-pitched nervous sound. Nash lets out a string of curse words. My face presses against the cement floor, where something tickles my nose. I smell grass. The weight lightens, and I open my eyes.

I sit in a small clearing, circled by trees. A disgusting and familiar stench makes me gag.

Then, it's pandemonium.

Mallory shrieks as a stream of oversize roaches scurry up her arms and legs. Ants bite Valeria, who spins and waves her arms and legs wildly to get them off. Sofia struggles to beat away screeching bats clutching and clawing at her hair. A large hairy black spider crawls on Nash's back. Rats close in on me, their mouths open, and I see blood on their teeth and whiskers.

Snakes hang by the hundreds from the trees, while ghostly humans with red eyes and red auras ride on horseback toward us. Everything glows through a blood-red filter, and it's all I can do not to puke my guts out.

Sofia grabs my arm and whimpers, "Where are we?" I shake my head and swipe at the bats in her hair.

I can't see Karl or Davon, and then I turn and find Karl in the center of the clearing. He stands in shock, his arms by his side, stiff as boards. Davon, who is behind Karl, picks up a rock and rushes in the direction of the horses.

151

"Finn," Nash screams. The spider has moved higher, toward his neck, its fat legs lifting up and down as it climbs. He pummels at it. "We're in the tapestry scene. We have to get out."

"What?" I yell. Rat bites send waves of pain up my legs.

I see Davon strike one of the shadowy riders with a rock, and the rider drops off its horse, as another rider sweeps by, knocking Karl to the ground. Karl falls on something, and I realize it's the dead man from the tapestry.

Nash is right. *Somehow, we're in the tapestry scene.* I wonder how he figured it out so fast.

The horse rears over Karl, and as it's about to trample him, Karl flails out, hitting the wooden object lying next to the corpse. A musical sound emerges, and it stops the horse in its tracks, like the freeze-frame of a video.

Karl picks up the object and begins to pluck the strings, slowly at first, and faster, until he's strumming. Colors shoot out with every chord. The red fog begins to dissipate.

The ground splits open beside Karl, and the dead man is the first to disappear into the rift. It widens. Nash runs to Karl, yanking him by the arm, both of them scuttling backwards to safety. Karl drags the musical object with him, continuing to play as grass from the clearing cascades into the hole.

I watch trees uproot, crashing into the gaping chasm. Snakes fly into the air like black curls, the bats right behind them, before they, too, are gone. The roaches fall from Mallory's limbs, their underbellies pale as milk, their legs waving as they sail by. The remaining red-eyed riders are bucked head-first off their horses and catapulted into the abyss. Their horses follow, braying in fear. Finally, the rats are sucked away from me, circling like water down a bathtub drain.

With a violent lurch, the classroom walls of Lionel's castle emerges, and the desks and chairs appear as if never disturbed. Lionel sits in his wheelchair, his expression unreadable, as Karl plucks a few more notes from the strange wooden object.

"Thank you, Karl. That will be enough," Lionel says.

We all gaze at each other in shocked silence.

"Dude," Nash yells. "That's what you call a little test? Haven't you ever heard of paper and pencil?"

"What happened to us?" Davon asks. He hits the side of his head and shakes it like he's trying to get water out of his ears.

"Karl has received his bequest," Lionel says.

"Are you for real?" Nash asks. "I can think of a lot of other ways to do that."

"Karl's bequest is a very special medieval instrument, sort of an early version of a guitar," Lionel replies, calmly. "It's called a psaltery."

"And giving it to him by putting us all in that tapestry was better than handing it to him because—?" Nash is furious, but Lionel continues to be unfazed by his outbursts.

"How did the psaltery music make the demons go away?" Mallory asks.

"It was invented to do so," Lionel says. "In Karl's hands now, it will be a powerful weapon."

"Did you invent it?" Mallory asks.

Lionel gazes at us before his eyes dart away. "That is a story for another time."

"What did you expect us to learn from that?"

Nash asks, still enraged.

"What do you think?"

Nash flexes the fingers of both hands, then squeezes them into fists.

"I think we learned to recognize demons," Davon says, after a sidelong glance at Nash.

"How?" Lionel asks.

"Because they look like what you told us— you know, bats, spiders, all that stuff," Davon replies.

"But there was something else," Sofia says. "Did anyone else see everything in red?"

"You mean like seeing through blood?" Valeria asks.

"I did," I say, sticking my hand up halfway.

After I raise my hand, Karl, Davon, and Mallory do, too.

"Professor Guillaume told us about the demons' red eyes. But, do demons have auras, like angels?" Mallory asks. "Red auras?"

"They do," Lionel says. "And we HALO angels are the only angels who have ever been able to see the red eyes and the red auras. We could not know for sure if you would be able to function as we do. That is another reason why I ran this simulation today. You were never in any real danger."

"You could have fooled me," Nash says, releasing his fists and laying his hands flat on his thighs.

"Did anyone have any other unusual experiences?" Lionel asks.

"If you mean, did it stink like a landfill, yes," Nash says.

Lionel presses his fingers together in a pyramid. "Anyone else, ah—smell anything?" Lionel asks.

We all assure him we did.

154

"Maggoty flesh," Karl says.

"I almost blew lunch," Davon adds.

"Are you telling us we're supposed to identify demons by their red eyes, red auras, and also by their *smell*?" Mallory asks, her voice rising.

"I am," Lionel says. "And now you have demonstrated the learning for today's lesson. Therefore, class is dismissed." He rolls his wheelchair backwards, a door opens up behind him, he rides through it, and abruptly, he is gone.

We are left to stare at one another in shock.

It takes us a few minutes to leave, and I am the last one out the door. I feel a compulsion to look back over my shoulder at the tapestry scene. It's exactly the same scene as it was at the beginning of class; a clearing surrounded by trees, soldiers on horseback, and a man right smack in the middle, lying still, his body covered in blood. I squint, trying to see if there's a difference.

Then I see it. The dead man's psaltery is gone.

Chapter 22
A Dream, a Dog, and a Destination

I dream again.

\ \ \ \ \ \ \

She's in trouble. I know where she is, and I have to get to her. I've figured out a way around the alarm; pretty brilliant if I do say so myself. I trick it by shielding through the door.

Once outside, I notice the smells first. They're intense: pine, old campfire ashes, and wild animals.

The building I came from is a log cabin. How clever. They change the building to fit the surroundings. I must be somewhere in the southwest. I hope it's not too far from where I need to go.

I rush away from the house, following a long

winding lane that cuts downhill between forests of scrub pine. At the end, I stand at the intersection of two roads, uncertain which way to go. I hear a sharp bark behind me. I turn around and see it's that dumb little dog. "Hey, get out of here!" I chase the dog a few feet back up the lane. "Go on, get." He retreats.

Back at the road, I turn left and jog a few hundred yards. I stop where a bridge arches over a stream, barely wide enough for a car to drive over. Beyond the bridge, the side of a hill is broken up by several cabins. The sign above the door of the biggest cabin says, **Crooked Creek Lodge***.*

Across the street from the lodge, a bar/restaurant is perched on the side of a hill. **Bronco Buck's Diner** *glows in large blue neon letters. The neon outline of a cowboy on horseback romps beside the restaurant's name, and a sign below says Payson, Arizona.*

An old man in a cowboy hat, muddy boots, jeans, and a flannel shirt walks out of the restaurant. He holds a cup of coffee with one hand and opens the door of a brand new truck with the other. **The Dancin' Ranch** *is written on the side of the truck. Sheesh. Everything has a name around here.*

"Hey," I say to the man. I step between him and the driver's seat. "Hey," I repeat, louder. I wave my hand in front of his face. He walks right through me, climbs in the truck, and slams the door.

Dude, this could be a problem.

I watch as he picks a cigar butt out of the ashtray, takes a square metal lighter out of his pocket, and clinks it open. He rolls his stubby finger along the top and a blue spark leaps into flame. The window opens, and the cigar sizzles as the man sucks in the smoke and blows it back out.

The man turns the key and cranks the engine. I see something move in the corner of my eye. It's the dog again. He jumps into the back of the pickup seconds before the driver jams the gearshift into reverse and backs out of the parking spot. The dog's nails scrabble on the metal as he tries to keep his footing.

I have no time to think. I grab the side of the pickup, place my foot on the bumper, hop up, and leap over. I land next to the little white dog. "You better know what you're doing, dog," I say.

We jostle and bounce for a few miles, and then the cowboy pulls into a parking lot full of pickups, RV's, and trailers. The parking lot circles a fenced-in dirt arena. A tiered grandstand, arranged in a semi-circle, connects each side of a metal gate, and behind the gates are pens full of animals. A billboard proclaims this to be **The World's Oldest Continuous Rodeo.**

Bareback riders circle the ring and wave their hats in the air. People shout. The air is full of the sweet smells of cotton candy, onion rings, and hotdogs slathered with ketchup and mustard.

I crawl out of the back of the truck. The dog trots along beside me as I walk up and down the rows, examining license plates. My head rises and falls like the noise of the crowd.

Impatient, I almost decide to try and follow signs to the highway, but I realize no one is going to stop and pick up an invisible hitchhiker. I kick the back of a large horse trailer in frustration, and the license plate is exactly what I am looking for.

I only have to wait a little while longer.

I sit on the top rung of the grimy fence. I have a great view, but this close, the stench of sheep, cow, and horse manure is overwhelming.

For the next few hours, I watch cowboys rope calves, race through a maze of barrels, and get bucked off wild horses. The clowns are my favorite, as they take their lives in their hands running in front of the animals.

The closing ceremony is awesome. The horses and their riders circle the ring at breakneck speed, and then one horse separates from the rest. The rider guides the horse's forelegs onto a tiny trampoline. The horse pauses for a moment as it pulls up its hind legs. The crowd roars as the rider's flag waves grandly in the wind. It's so cool.

By dark, I lie in the empty stall of a double horse trailer, headed for California. The dog sleeps at my feet. When the vehicle stops, hours later, I hop out.

It takes me a little while to locate the hospital, and even longer to find the room, but once I stand in the small curtained space, I gaze at the pretty girl with intense longing. Her strawberry blond hair splays out on the pillow of the bed. The place smells like alcohol and urine, but she smells familiar, like salt water.

A woman wearing scrubs walks in, checks a line, adjusts a few knobs, and wraps a blood pressure cuff around the girl's arm. As the cuff contracts, I check the girl's chart. The numbers and scrawled notes mean nothing to me. I don't know what I thought I'd understand.

I hear someone clear his throat behind me. I turn my head in the direction of the sound, and I see an elderly couple hovering a few inches from the ceiling in the corner of the room. "We've been expecting you," the old man says. His white hair sticks out in tufts, and he wears an old army uniform. "You better hide."

"What? Why would I do that?" I reply.

"Because you're in danger," the old lady says, her lips tightening into a thin line. She wears a faded cotton dress, pearls, and a pair of thick-heeled shoes. "You can be sure that HE will be sending someone."

I think of a smart remark, when the dog, which has never left my side, starts to growl. I sniff the odor of rotting meat and hear a strange whistling noise just outside the curtain. The hair on my arms and the back of my neck starts to fizz like a soft drink.

"You know how to shield, don't you son?" the old man asks.

"I would do it quickly then, dear," the old lady says.

I look around wildly for someplace to hide, and

then I dive into the cabinet beside the hospital bed. At the last second, I remember to close my eyes.

＼ ＼ ＼ ＼ ＼ ＼ ＼

I wake. I'm surprised to find myself in my bed at HALO's dormitory. The room is so bright it looks like a black and white photograph, all harsh angles and shadows, and I pull the covers up over my eyes to block out the light.

I can't remember what I dreamed, but I know from the way my stomach feels, it was something really bad.

Kip Taylor

Day 5

Remember upon the conduct of each depends the fate of all.

-Alexander the Great

Kip Taylor

Chapter 23
Quite a Bit of Worry

"Hey, where's Nash?" Davon asks.

"He's probably going to be late again," Mallory says. "I think he enjoys making the rest of us wait."

Seminar is about to begin. We're sitting around shooting the breeze.

"He wasn't in the room when I got up this morning," I say. "His bike is gone, so he's probably out for a ride."

"He was in pretty bad shape when he went to bed," Valeria remarks, biting her thumbnail.

"He was asleep when I got to our room" I say. "I think Mallory's right. He's trying to make a point."

"Why don't you go find him," Rouena says to me. She waves her hand toward the door casually, but her eyes look worried. "We can't allow him to think he can be late for his responsibilities. Try any place you think he may have gone. We'll get started without you."

I dash back to the dorm, where I check all the rooms and the back yard. I think about walking to the other side of the lake to the A-frame that has such a strange draw for me, but I change my mind. It looks deserted. I hop on my bike and ride out to the place where Nash and I hung out the first day after we got here. I yell his name, but he's not there. I even ride back to Lionel's castle, looking up and down the stream from the bridge. Finally, I search behind all the cottages on both sides of the main street.

I figure I must have missed him, so I return to Welcome Cottage and lean my bike against the front porch. When I go inside, everyone, including Claude, Avery, and all of the instructors, is standing by the fireplace, but there is no sign of Nash.

Claude looks terrible. His eyes are black coals, his suit is rumpled, and his hair seems to have gone gray overnight.

"It appears that I have sent you on a wild goose chase, Finn," Rouena says. "We may have underestimated how disturbed Nash has been about being here."

I perch on the arm of the couch, next to Sofia. I hear a sharp intake of breath. Valeria is crying.

"Claude believes he may know how Nash got off the grounds," Lionel says.

Claude's voice lacks its usual cheery tone. "Since you arrived, we have been moving the school from place to place for safety." He bunches his tie with his hand, smoothing it back out and bunching it again. "When we picked you up, we were in Colorado, and we have since moved to Japan, then to Greece, and then back to the United States. The alarm system has been active the entire time."

Rouena cuts in. "Unfortunately, we think that Nash used his talent to circumvent the alarm system."

"You mean you know what his talent is?" Mallory asks.

"We know what all of your talents are," Rouena says. "Nash has the ability to solve problems, even the most complex. He visited Claude yesterday morning, which was why he came to history class late. He picked up enough information about our alarm system to outsmart it."

Claude hangs his head. He looks so distraught that I go to him, crouch down, and put my arm around his shoulders.

"It's not your fault, Claude," I say.

"Of course not, Claude," Rouena agrees. "We believe Nash started to plan this escape a couple of days ago. Last night, he slipped downstairs, shielded through the front door, and found himself in Arizona."

Shielded through the front door. Arizona. Something about this is familiar.

"But, why?" Avicenne asks. She leans against Theo.

"It may have something to do with the fact that he opened a portal in Council Cottage yesterday morning," Lionel says.

"He knows how to open a portal?" Sofia asks. "But, we haven't learned that yet."

"He watched me do it twice," Rouena says. "For Nash, that would be enough."

"And now he could be anywhere on earth," Avery says, his voice trembling. "Vulnerable to who knows what." He cracks his knuckles, and I cringe.

"It wasn't your fault either, Avery," Professor Guillaume says.

"No, It wasn't," I say, releasing Claude and standing. "If anyone knew how he felt, it was me. I'm his roommate. I should have said something to one of you. He must have told me a million times he didn't want any of this responsibility."

Feelings of déjà vu swirl in my mind, flitting too fast to pin down. I do know how Nash feels. I know *exactly* how Nash feels.

"We all knew he was upset, Finn," Valeria says.

"Yes, we did," Rouena says. She throws her hands up in the air. "It's nobody's fault, except Nash's. He has put us all at risk."

"I'm afraid I have to throw in another monkey wrench," Avicenne says. "Unless..." Her eyes sweep the room. "Well, have any of you seen Riley? He usually hangs out with me every morning in the Infirmary, but I haven't seen him today."

"My Riley?" I ask.

The swirling feelings stop. Instead, my thoughts become insistent strikes. *Riley. And. Nash. Something. Important.* If only I can remember.

"I think Riley may be with Nash," Avicenne says.

"And Nash is probably going to find Jordana, wherever she is," Karl says. "That's what I would do.

Nash. And. Jordana. A memory blasts through. *Nash in a hospital room with Jordana.*

"I checked on Jordana a little while ago," says Lionel. "Nash isn't there."

I cover my head with my hands and sink to my knees. Claude pats me on the back. "There, there, Master Finn. What's wrong?"

Sofia flies over to crouch beside me. "Finn, what is it?"

"Lionel's wrong," I blurt. "Nash is there."

Sofia puts her hands on my cheeks and turns my face toward hers. "What are you talking about?"

"Finn, Nash doesn't even know where Jordana is," Lionel says. "Jordana isn't at home or at school, or any of the normal places she hangs out."

"I know," I say. My voice creeps higher. "She's in the hospital."

"How could you know that?" Theo asks. "Unless—"

"I was with him when he got there. I mean, it was like I was him. I left with him. We shielded out the door. And you're right, Avicenne. Riley was there. Nash was mad about it."

Sofia puts her arm around my back and pulls me down on the carpet beside her.

"Tell us what else you remember, Finn," she says.

"We, I mean Nash, got a ride in a horse trailer all the way to California. He found the hospital. He's with Jordana, right now. That's what I'm trying to tell you. Nash is in Jordana's hospital room." A sickening feeling jabs me in the gut. "He's in trouble, too. Some old people were telling him to hide."

"Finn is describing the Peekers," says Professor Guillaume. "They're Jordana's guardians."

"If what you're telling us is true, Finn, then I'm afraid we've got to act fast," Rouena says. "Nash is in grave danger."

Chapter 24
A Plan

"He must have found out about Jordana when he opened the portal, yesterday," Lionel says.

"It doesn't matter," Rouena says. "The damage has been done. How much time do we have?"

"Only a few hours, I'm afraid," Lionel replies. "Finn's lagtime."

"My what?" I ask.

"Your lagtime. It's the time when what *you* call dreaming-the-events occur and when the events actually occur," Rouena says. "Right now, Nash is probably in that horse trailer you mentioned."

I have more questions—like what the heck is she talking about, but Rouena gets down to business, barking orders at us. The instructors have already left to do whatever they need to do. "Claude, get us to San Diego, pronto. Avery, go with him and help with the preparations." She turns to us. "Fledglings," she says, "go get whatever you think may help, especially any bequests we've given you. And, for goodness sake, don't dawdle."

A few minutes later, I lose my balance and fall against the wall in Nash's and my room. Claude is moving us. I can't find anything helpful to bring, so I wait for Karl and Davon in the great room. Karl appears, carrying the psaltery, and Davon wears the hauberk and smock.

"It's a good thing one of us had the dream about Nash," I say, as we hurry toward Welcome Cottage.

"What do you mean?" Davon asks.

"I'm glad I remembered where Nash went," I say.

"I've never had a dream like that," Karl says.

"I dream, but they're dumb dreams, nothing like yours," Davon says. "And I've never dreamed I was somebody else."

"You haven't?" I ask.

"Nope—never gone anywhere I haven't been either," Karl says.

"I thought everybody dreamed they were other people," I say. "I've done it all my life. I can't be the only one."

"Maybe you are," Karl says. "Maybe that's your talent."

"Hey, cool, Finn," Davon says. "I bet Karl's right." He and Karl high-five each other.

"Did you tell your parents?" Karl asks.

"Sure," I say. "They said I had a vivid imagination."

The guys burst out laughing.

We reach Welcome Cottage, where Rouena

waits alone by the fireplace. The girls arrive a few minutes later. Valeria has her medicine bag, and Mallory carries the leather satchel with the copy of *Beowulf*. Sofia, like me, is empty-handed.

"I thought about bringing a paintbrush," Sofia says. "But I didn't know how that would help."

"Finn, thank you for finding Nash," Valeria says, chewing on her thumbnail. "We're lucky you have this dreaming talent, aren't we?"

Lionel rolls in, holding a book. I feel another jolt. I grab the back of the couch with one hand and reach out my other to steady Sofia.

"Rouena, why is Nash in grave danger?" Sofia asks.

"Yeah, why can't Nash visit Jordana for a little while and get it out of his system?" Mallory asks. "He might be easier to get along with if he did."

"Nash is no longer in the safe environment of HALO," Lionel interjects. "General Jarray will be sending someone for him, if he doesn't come himself."

"Who's General Jarray?" Valeria asks.

I remember Professor Guillaume mentioning his name once, and I think maybe one of the Peekers mentioned it, too, in my dream.

Rouena doesn't sugarcoat it. "General Jarray is the head of the most powerful demon army on earth. He is HALO's greatest enemy, and he has known for many years about *The Thousand Year Change*. He worked hard to find out who our fledglings would be." She bites her lip.

"But we cannot protect you from him when you are outside of HALO," Lionel says.

Theo and Avicenne arrive together, toting a jeweled box. Professor Guillaume turns up last. He has a large rolled-up poster jammed under his arm, and he arranges all of us around the coffee table.

"We have devised a plan for you," Lionel begins.

"For us?" Mallory asks. "Aren't you going?"

"No, Mallory," Rouena says. "We can't."

"But I thought you said it was unsafe for us to be outside of HALO," Sofia says.

"That is true," Professor Guillaume says. He takes his pipe out and taps it on his palm. Changing his mind, he slides his pipe back in his pocket again. "Here is the problem. We are in the final phase of our existence. In fact, the only one among us who is capable of earth visits anymore is Maddelena. You have to think of us as, well, elderly. We haven't got the energy to go to earth anymore. We must use all our remaining energy to teach you."

"I don't understand," Valeria says.

"What I mean is, you have to go to earth to retrieve Nash yourselves," the professor says.

"But what about the field trip?" I ask. "You and Rouena were both with us at Wyattholme."

Was that really only yesterday? Rouena saved us by opening a portal, and Professor Guillaume used who-knows-what powers to save that peasant woman. How are we going to get Nash back without help from our instructors? Only some of us know our talents and have bequests, the only skill we know is how to shield, and we don't even have our wings yet.

"The field trip was not the same," Rouena says. "That was travel to a past time. The energy used was minimal, and we planned for it."

"Even so," Professor Guillaume says, "with the events that occurred in the church, Avicenne had to work her magic on Rouena and me to get us back up to speed."

The instructors must be a lot more fragile than they look or act. My heart sinks as I realize how much Nash has really screwed things up. How could he be so stupid? And then, I think of Sofia.

"We don't all have to go, do we?" I ask. "Couldn't the girls stay back?"

"Why would we do that?" Mallory asks, looking annoyed. "I'm going."

"Me too," Valeria says.

"Me too, Finn," Sofia says. "I'm going wherever you're going."

Suddenly I feel lightheaded. "Is it warm in here?" I ask.

"The first rule of our plan is—" Rouena's voice falters. "—it's that you must all stick together."

"What if demons show up while we're there?" Davon asks.

Lionel interrupts. "Let's not borrow trouble."

Rouena nods. "Yes. If there are no further questions then, Lionel?"

"Jordana is at Scripps Mercy Hospital," Lionel says. "I've spoken to the Peekers. They're on the alert for Nash's arrival. They will protect him to the utmost of their abilities until you get there. I am confident they will do The Old Guard proud."

"The Old Guard?" Davon asks. "Who are they?"

"One of the most respected of the angel communities," Lionel answers. "Our very own retirement village."

"That's who is guarding Jordana?" Mallory asks, incredulous. "Retirees?"

"Members of The Old Guard are hardly typical retirees, Mallory," Professor Guillaume interjects. "They are experienced and savvy angels, most of them highly decorated."

It makes me wonder who is guarding my dad.

"What happened to Jordana?" Valeria asks.

"She almost drowned yesterday," Lionel says. "She's in a coma. It's not supposed to be her time, so she may pull through. But Nash had no way of knowing that yesterday morning when he overheard the doctor, who was telling her parents it was touch and go. I believe the direct quote was, 'We don't know how much damage there was to her brain while she was under water.'"

No wonder Nash was even more of a basket case yesterday.

"Did a demon try to drown Jordana?" Sofia asks.

Rouena beams at Sofia. "You are beginning to think like an angel, Sofia," she says. "The demons at work here are shrewd. They know the value of a HALO fledgling, and they would try anything to force one of you to come to them."

"Well, it sure worked," Mallory says, pushing her glasses up and crossing her arms.

"Are demons trying to get to our families, too?" Sofia asks in a nervous voice.

"Your families and friends are being looked after," Rouena says. "Don't worry."

Lionel nudges the professor. "Guillaume? The plan?"

"Theo and I have mapped a strategy," the professor says. "Each of you will have a specific job. Finn, you are in charge of the operation, from the time

175

we release you in San Diego until such time as you return."

Me? In charge? While I recover from this surprising bit of news, Professor Guillaume takes the roll of paper from under his arm and spreads it on the table. "We are here," he says, tapping a wooden pointer over a spot on the chart paper. A city map appears. "This is about a block away from the hospital. You will walk out this door and along this sidewalk." He slides the pointer along a couple of streets, and then he stops and raps the same spot several times. "Use this entrance to the hospital."

The professor hands the pointer to Theo. Theo smacks the pointer on the paper, the street map disappears, and a blueprint of the hospital emerges. "Once inside," Theo says, "you must go straight to Jordana's room, which is on the third floor in the Intensive Care Unit. The ICU is an open ward, with patient cubicles circling the nurses' station in the center. Each patient cubicle is cordoned off from the other by walls and a curtain, and all patients are monitored twenty-four hours a day."

Professor Guillaume rolls up the chart paper. Lionel pulls out the book he brought, and I bend my head sideways to read the title. Strategic Warfare for Guardian Angels, by Theodopolous Costalides.

"Hey, did you write this, Theo?" Davon asks.

"It's merely a draft," Theo says. He takes the book from Lionel, opens it, and reads several excerpts from a chapter titled, "Retrieval of Fugitives, Mavericks, and Renegades," assigning each of us a responsibility as he goes along. "If you follow the plan," he remarks after he snaps the book shut, "it should work like a well-oiled machine."

Lionel adds a warning as we stand to go. "If at any time you see red eyes or red auras, or if you smell what you suspect may be a demon, by all means abandon the plan and get out of there."

Claude appears at the door. He has changed his suit and tie, and he seems to have revived a bit. "The exit is ready," he says. He bows to us. "My dear fledglings," he continues. "I am confident you will be successful in your endeavor."

"Wait," Theo says. "We have one more thing to give you." He and Avicenne hoist the jeweled box onto the table. Theo unhooks the lid, reaches in, and takes out a small pipe-shaped object with a fleur-de-lis design at the top. It almost looks like a wand, but it's thicker and heavier. Theo hands it to me.

"In an absolute emergency," Theo says. "This will call Maddelena to you. Use it wisely, as it has only one call left."

"How?" I ask.

"Bend the leaves down," Theo says.

"Bend iron?"

Is he kidding me?

"Ask Davon to help you," Theo says, and he winks at me.

"Follow me, ladies and gentlemen," Claude announces.

I trudge over the grassy hill and drag myself down the stairs, lagging behind the group. As I glance behind me, I see the sonnet. Two of the lines are glowing.

...It is for you to find what must be done,
To breach the wall and slay the ready foe,

I feel an overwhelming sense of doom.

When we reach the first floor, it looks nothing like the cavernous room I remember. Instead, it is an office full of cubicles. Dozens of human workers answer phones and scurry back and forth. Beyond the windows, a busy city street hums with moving cars and strolling pedestrians.

"Remember, they can't see you," Claude says, ushering us through the mayhem to a revolving front door. He pats us each on the back and shouts, "Good luck!" as we stumble through the heavy rotating doors two at a time—Mallory and me first, Sofia and Valeria second, and Karl and Davon bringing up the rear.

We spill out into the haze of polluted city air, and the hot pavement burns under my feet. I rattle off the plan again as we hurry toward the hospital.

Chapter 25
A Plan Goes South

We climb the stairs to the third floor of the hospital, push through a set of double doors, and the first thing I see is Riley sprinting down the hallway toward us. "Riley. Good boy. Have you been taking care of Nash? Where is he, boy? Can you show us?" Riley cocks his head to the left and right as he listens to me. Then he spins in circles and tears back down the hallway, toward another set of doors. "Whoa, wait up," I yell.

Still nervous, I run through the plan a final time. It's basically a quick grab. "Karl, you and Davon stay by the nurses' station. Karl, be prepared to play the psaltery, if necessary. Mallory, your post is right outside the curtain." I figure the less contact Mallory and Nash have, the better. "Valeria, Sofia, and I will go in and get Nash."

When we get to the ICU, Karl, Davon, and

Mallory take their places, and I push the curtain aside. Valeria's job is to assess Nash's health, but since he's still shielding, she immediately rushes to Jordana's side. "Do you see? The light around her body is blue, but her head is white."

"Sorry, Val, I don't' see anything," Sofia says. Her job is to keep watch inside the cubicle and to warn me of anything out of the ordinary.

I get ready to call Nash out of the cabinet.

"Psssssst." A noise comes from the ceiling.

I gaze up. "Hello? Is that you, Mr. Peeker?" I ask.

"No." A little old lady appears out of the gray gloom. "It's me." She looks exactly as she did in my dream, like somebody's tiny plump grandmother in a flowered housecoat and comfortable shoes, except now I can see she has a beautiful set of wings. They are not full length. She is a hundred-year angel, like Claude and Avery. Beside her, a white-haired gentleman appears, wearing a World War I uniform with medals on his chest.

"Hello, young man," the soldier says, his wings fluttering. "You must be Mr. Flanagan."

"And you must be Mr. and Mrs. Peeker," I reply.

"The very same," the little old lady says. "I'm Betty, and this is Sergeant Raymond, but everyone calls him Snorty because of his—"

"Betty, dear, it's not the time," the old man says, placing a hand gently on her arm. He turns back to me. "You must flush the renegade out of hiding, and then you must make a swift and strategic retreat. The enemy has sent reconnaissance, and the troops will be along soon."

"Thank you," I say. "We'll get Nash and go, then."

I turn around; facing the cabinet where Nash is shielding. As I prepare to execute my part of the plan, I get distracted. Valeria is leaning over the bed, stroking Jordana's forehead, when her hands start to shimmer. I watch as she closes her eyes and moves her hands to Jordana's neck. A bright green light begins to pulse from Valeria's hands. Jordana's neck begins to glow the color blue, and the color slowly slides along Jordana's jaw, up over her cheeks and across her forehead.

After a few moments, Valeria's hands go back to normal and she pulls them back. Jordana's head radiates blue a few moments longer, and then the color fades away.

"Sofia," Valeria says, rolling her shoulders and shaking her head. "My back itches right here." She lifts her arm and points. "Will you scratch it, please?"

I have no idea what Valeria did to Jordana and no time to think about it. "Samuel Nash Anthony," I bellow in my most authoritative voice. "We know you're in there. We've come to take you back to HALO, and we're not leaving without you, so you might as well come on out."

Jordana twitches and moans.

"Oh, look," Valeria says. "Jordana's waking up."

I hear Nash stir in the cabinet as Jordana opens her eyes and stretches her arms. "Mom? Dad?" she asks. "Is anybody here?"

Nash rockets from his hiding place.

"Nash, look. Valeria did something that healed Jordana," Sofia says.

Nash shoves past me and leans over the bed.

"Jordana? Jordana? It's me, Nash. Are you okay?"

"You know she can't see or hear you, Nash," I say. "I'm sorry."

Nash squeezes Jordana's hand, and then he straightens up, turns to Valeria, and throws his arms around her neck. "Valeria, you brought her back. I thought she was going to die. Thank you. Thank you."

Valeria pushes Nash out arms' length and examines him. "I didn't do anything, really, Nash."

Nash breaks Valeria's hold and turns back toward Jordana. He runs his hand along Jordana's cheek and strokes her hair.

"C'mon, Nash. We have to go," I say.

"Dude, I can't go now. I came all this way. I have to tell her—can I be alone with her for a minute?"

"Seriously?" I ask. "Do you have any idea how much danger you've put yourself in, not to mention the rest of us who had to come to earth and rescue you?"

"Finn," Sofia says, tugging softly on my arm. She tiptoes up to whisper in my ear. "Maybe we could let him have one minute. We can wait outside the curtain. The Peekers will still be here, right?"

My stomach tightens. It's not in the plan, but it's hard for me to say no to Sofia.

"I know it's what I would want," Sofia says. I can feel her warm breath on my cheek.

I cave. "Okay. You have one minute, Nash," I say. "And don't make me come back in here for you."

I guide Sofia and Valeria out of the curtained cubicle and tell them to wait with Karl and Davon over by the nurses' station. I stand close to the curtain with Mallory. I tap my foot and bite my cuticles, counting the seconds as they tick by. The only hint I get that things are about to go terribly wrong is a whiff of the now-familiar fetid odor of rotting meat.

I have made a huge mistake.

I burst through the curtain to Jordana's room just in time to see Sergeant Peeker, his white hair flying, riding piggy-back on a woman in a nurse's uniform. The nurse tries to buck him off, and for a fleeting moment, the scene is hilarious. But this is not a real nurse, it's a shape-shifting demon, and this situation is the opposite of funny.

After a few moments of frantic movement, the nurse lookalike falls, bounces off the end of Jordana's bed, and sprawls onto the floor with a thud.

"I've got your back, Snorty," Betty screams. She stomps on the demon's head with her orthopedic shoes. A sickening crack reverberates throughout the room, and the demon nurse's head begins to liquefy, seeping into the floor.

The nurse vanishes.

"Go," Betty cries. She points to Nash. "Take that one and go!"

Before I can grab Nash, a brawny bald man, with tattoos covering his entire head and body, storms out of the corner. He opens his mouth and emits a foul black smoke. The entire room goes dark, and I cough and gag. I can't see Nash. I can only hear him and the Peekers choking, too.

One of the Peekers clears the air with a furious blast of wings. Then I see the Sergeant point at the tattooed demon. His finger emits an electrical charge like lightening, and the demon falls, but not before firing off another round of sooty, lung-clogging smoke.

I grab a handful of what I hope is Nash's t-shirt, and squinting through the tears streaming from my irritated eyes, reach out wildly for the curtain. Suddenly, a ball of flame erupts behind us.

"*Run!*" Sergeant Peeker shouts.

I crash through the curtain, looking back for a split second as the ball of flame and both of the Peekers disappear into the wall. Fabric rips, and Nash topples to the floor, his legs still inside Jordana's room. I'm left holding a piece of Nash's t-shirt.

Nash screams, and I turn. Dark slime bubbles up from the floor. I fall to my hands and knees. The slime covers Nash's legs, and the steaming stench burns my nostrils. I manage to grab one of Nash's arms. I pull with all my strength and shout for help.

Davon is the first to arrive. He lunges past, and without a moment's hesitation, pounces on top of the green mound. Pounding his fists, he shrieks, "Let go! Let go!"

Karl grabs Nash's other arm. We strain, but Nash is still caught in the monster's vise-like grip.

"We're losing him. Use the fleur-de-lis to call Maddelena!" Mallory wails, and I see a tentacle shoot by, curling around Mallory and flinging her over the nurses' station to the opposite side of the ICU, where she crashes into a closet door and slides down to the floor, groaning.

The slime creeps up Nash's torso, and soon the liquid acid melts the flesh off my hands so I have to let go. Karl releases Nash, too, and we roll on the floor in pain.

"Stay away!" I manage to hiss to Sofia and Valeria. Then I try to pull the fleur-de-lis from my pocket with my damaged hands. I tug too hard, and it skitters across the room, coming to rest under Jordana's bed, useless.

I watch helplessly as Nash's head dissolves into

the slime, which explodes like a Puffer fish and begins to shake. It jumps, crashing through the window of Jordana's hospital room. I see Davon flip into the air above it.

I struggle to my feet and run to the open window. Three stories below, Davon sprawls on the grass in his armor, without a scratch.

No trace is left of the demon or Nash.

Kip Taylor

Day 6

If one looks closely enough, one can see angels in every piece of art.

-Adeline Cullen Ray

Kip Taylor

Chapter 26
Mysterious Painting

The instructors leave us alone.

Sofia tells us the only way she can deal with her feelings is to paint, so she goes to her studio. The rest of us can't seem to stand to be apart, and we follow her. No one has talked about what happened yet. No one wants to bring it up. The rescue attempt was a disaster, and Nash's fate is unknown.

Searching for a comfortable position on one of the futons, I pull one leg up, lay it back down, and then do the same with the other. Davon lies with me, his head at the other end and his feet beside my chest. Karl stretches out on the other futon, Riley curled at his side. Valeria and Mallory sit cross-legged on the floor, half-heartedly playing cards.

I watch Sofia paint. Avicenne has healed my burns, but nothing can heal my depression. I am drowning in self-pity. I was in charge, and I failed.

"Davon, Avicenne told us that you didn't have a scratch on you," Sofia says. Brush in hand, she steps back to view her work. "I guess that armor really works."

"You bet it does," Davon says. "But I would gladly give it to any of you if I thought it would help get Nash back."

"Nope. It only works for you," Karl says, shaking his head. "At least, I think I remember Theo saying that."

"I wish I could have seen you beating up that demon," Valeria says. "That must have been something."

"It was pure courage," Karl says.

"Maybe if I hadn't let go of the fleur-de-lis," I say, "things would have turned out better."

"You don't know that," Karl says, scratching behind Riley's ears absentmindedly.

"Well, at least you proved you're the healer, Valeria," Mallory says. "Not that we doubted it."

"Yes," Sofia says. "You were amazing. One minute Jordana was in a coma, and the next, she was fine." She smiles at Valeria. "Healed by the touch of your hands."

"It was so strange," Valeria says, "because I hardly felt as if I did anything." She picks up a card, glances at it, and lays the same card back down on the pile.

"You're being modest," Mallory says, plucking Valeria's card from the top of the pile.

"Yes, you are, Valeria," Sofia says. "I can't imagine having ability like that."

"You know," Mallory says, changing the subject, "if that cheeky Nash was here, I bet he'd be asking whether that demon throwing me into a wall knocked any sense into me."

Karl grins. "Yep. He would definitely say something like that."

"I hate to admit it," Mallory continues, "but I miss him. At the same time I want to punch him, of course."

Davon turns on his side, gazing up at Sofia and squinting in the light. "Sofia, what are you painting, anyway?"

"I'm not really sure. Sometimes, especially when I'm in here, I get an idea, but it's like the brush has a mind of its own. I end up with something completely different than what I planned."

"You don't mind us all being here, do you?" I ask.

Sofia flashes her perfect teeth. "Of course, not, Finn." She leans back again, dabs her brush in color, and pats the canvas with it again and again. "I'm glad you're here. I need you. All of you."

I know what she means. The people in this room are like the brothers and sisters I never had. Except Sofia, of course. I don't think of her like a sister. Not even close.

Though I'm still upset, I feel a bit better since we've started to talk about what happened.

A girlish shriek jolts me upright. "Where did you get a picture of Sweyn?" Avery stands at the door to the studio, pointing to Sofia's canvas with one hand and covering his mouth with the other.

"Did I do something wrong?" Sofia asks. Her face crumples.

I scramble up from the futon and stand by her side. "Avery, you're scaring Sofia," I say.

"But, it's Sweyn!" Avery shouts, waving his hands in frenzy. "I can hardly believe my eyes. How did you get him so exactly right?" He walks toward Sofia's canvas. Instinctively, I stand in front of it and her.

"Sweyn? You mean the instructor we've never met?" I ask.

"Yes," he says. He drops his hands. "Sweyn is Maddelena's partner. The two of them are the most powerful HALO angels. But Sweyn was kidnapped. It's the great tragedy of HALO's existence."

"Kidnapped?" I ask.

Avery doesn't answer me. He stares at the painting. "Sofia, my little bird, how could you know what he looks like? His picture was not with the others in the dormitory."

"I don't know," Sofia responds. "He was—just there in my head."

"The instructors have to see this," Avery says. He backs up to the door, still gaping wide-eyed at the painting of Sweyn. As he leaves, I hear him mutter, "Oh, dear. Oh, dear. Wait until they see this."

I pat Sofia's arm as we all crowd around the canvas and examine her painting. Sweyn is a striking angel, dressed in a billowing white shirt and lace-up boots over old-fashioned tights. He lies against a wall of bars, his eyes closed, his wings grazing the dirty floor.

A shiver runs up the back of my neck and peace seeps deep into my bones, a feeling which I have gotten only twice before, around Maddelena. Then I study the painting, and through the bars, I see boxes with writing on them. The detail astonishes me. "This painting is unbelievable, Sofia," I say.

"Yeah, the way he looks—he's amazing," Karl says.

"So handsome," Mallory adds.

Murmurs of assent come from Valeria and Davon. Even Riley barks.

"But, what does this mean?" Sofia asks in a trembling voice. "How could I paint someone I've never even seen?"

Chapter 27
Behind the Boxes

Avery carries the painting to Council Cottage and sets it on its easel near the door. Rouena, Professor Guillaume, and Theo huddle in front of it, and a feverish discussion takes place over the next few minutes. The six of us fledglings wait, fidgeting nearby.

Claude hovers outside as Avery comes in and whispers something into Rouena's ear. Then Avery joins Claude again, and they rush away.

"He looks so ill," I hear Theo say in a low voice. "I hope Avicenne—"

Rouena cuts him off. "Obviously, it's a message from Sweyn himself; sent to us through Sofia. What we are supposed to do with it is the question." This causes a fresh batch of murmuring among the three instructors.

Lionel rolls in and breaks up the private conference. "Maddelena will be with us when she can," he says. "She has been seeing to the Peekers and notifying the other communities of the latest news."

Before I can even think the words fly out of my mouth. "The Peekers? Are they all right?" A vision of the elderly couple being flung around Jordana's hospital room blazes before me.

"They were badly hurt," Lionel says. "But Maddelena has managed to return them to their community, and Avicenne is tending to them."

"That's a relief," Valeria says.

Mallory raises her hand. "When are you going to tell us about Sweyn?"

"Yes, Mallory. It's time," Rouena answers. She gestures toward the round meeting table. "Here, why don't you all sit?"

We pull our chairs up to the table. Theo slides the painting closer, and then he, Professor Guillaume, and Lionel continue to scrutinize it. The professor pulls out a large magnifying glass, which he begins to use to examine every inch of the painting while Rouena brings us up to date.

"Sweyn was captured by General Jarray decades ago," Rouena says in a voice both sad and angry. "He was on a rare solo mission for HALO in Germany, identifying demons within Hitler's army."

From what I know of Hitler and his army, I wonder how any one of them *wasn't* a demon.

"From all reports," Rouena continues, "it seems Sweyn was trying to save a trainload of Jewish prisoners on their way to extermination in a concentration camp. The courageous and successful effort took every ounce of power he had, and for a few moments afterward, Sweyn was in a position of weakness. Jarray and his demons swept in and captured him." She drops her voice. "We have never been able to find him."

"Can an angel be killed?" Sofia asks. I know she is also asking what all of us need to know. *Has Nash been killed?*

"It takes a great deal of effort for an angel to fight a demon when it tries to steal its life force, so if it is close enough to its time, an angel can go to its reward, the Light, to escape," Rouena says. "Sweyn is close now, but not when he was taken. We have worried that he could be tortured to a point where he was too weak to resist anymore."

Tortured? Is Nash being tortured? Doesn't he have a thousand years of life force left?

Suddenly, Professor Guillaume whirls around. "Attention," he yells, waving the magnifying glass wildly. "I need everyone's attention immediately." The light from the magnifying glass bounces off the walls in narrow rays. "First, I have certified that this is, in fact, our Sweyn. If I may point out...can you see?" He points to Sweyn's left hand. "The Ring of Paladin."

"What's that?" Mallory asks.

"It was Sweyn's bequest from the Light Spirits," Rouena informs us. She is smiling. "Thank you, Sofia. You have brought us the best news we could possibly receive. Sweyn is alive, and he is still a HALO angel."

The professor holds up his hand for our attention. "It is my opinion that this painting shows where Sweyn is being kept prisoner. Finn? Could you come here for a moment? I need your eyes."

"Sure," I answer, still troubled about Nash. How could he resist demons' torture for a thousand years? I can't see how it would be possible. I push my chair back, get up, and stride across to the other side of the table.

"What do you see, right there?" Professor Guillaume asks, handing me the magnifying glass and pointing to a group of boxes in the background of the painting.

I grasp the magnifying glass and peer through it. The professor guides my hand to a spot, and that's when I barely make out an address label on one of the boxes. I squint as hard as I can, and I can just read it. "J.R. Antiquities," I say. "10 West 25th St., New York, New York, 10001."

"I thought so," Guillaume says. "An address, but more importantly, a name." His face falls. "Unfortunately, I think this is one of General Jarray's companies."

"Yes, yes, I think you're on to something, Guillaume," Lionel says.

"What makes you think so?" Rouena asks. She seems nervous.

"As you know, Jarray has an incarnation on earth as a highly successful English antiques merchant by the name of James Randolph," Lionel says. "I would say J.R. and Antiquities fits the bill, wouldn't you, Rouena?"

I tune them out and go back to perusing the painting with the magnifying glass. I stop and go back over a blurry object, which appears in the background between two of the larger boxes. Something about it is familiar. My eyes strain, and choppy blond hair, and a torn gray t-shirt that I know has StokerBoker surf on it, snaps into focus. "Shut up," I blurt.

"What?" Rouena asks.

"It's Nash." I poke the painting with my finger. "See, right here. It's Nash." I punch the air with my fist, magnifying glass and all. Then I drop the glass on the table, run to Sofia, pick her up right out of her chair and swing her around. "You found Nash, too, Sof!" I yell. "You found him."

"Group hug," Mallory shouts, as she, Davon, Karl, and Valeria join us. We jump up and down and laugh like lunatics.

Theo pulls out a chair, climbs up, places his fingers between his lips and whistles. We all fall silent. "Over here, please," he says.

I hear the door of Council Cottage squeak open. Avery and Claude are wrestling their way through with the Trunk of Kings, the same trunk which had Davon's hauberk and smock and Riley's vest in it. It strikes me how different the two assistant angels are; one tall and thin, dressed outrageously in a brown and black striped suit and leopard-print shoes, the other short and stocky, his suit a conservative navy blue.

Claude carries most of the weight, the trunk sloping down in his direction. They stumble to the front of the painting, and Avery drops his side first, where it thuds onto the floor. Claude sets his side down gently, and then they retreat to a position by the door.

Avicenne appears between the two sentinels. "Gentlemen," she says to Claude and Avery, nodding as she skips through. Theo hops off the chair and rushes to her side. "Avi, you're back. We'll have to catch you up." They hug. "Any chance Maddelena will make it?"

Avicenne shakes her head and makes a beeline for the painting. The rest of the instructors gather with her, behind the trunk. Professor Guillaume and Theo whisper together for a few moments, and then Theo opens the lid, reaches into the trunk, and brings out a small wooden box.

"Sofia, will you please join us?" Rouena says.

Sofia glances at me in surprise before stepping up to the trunk. I shrug and smile proudly.

Theo hands the small wooden box to Rouena, who takes the top off and shows its contents to Sofia.

Sofia reaches in and extracts a large locket with a delicate long gold chain that spills gracefully over her fingers. "It's exquisite." She holds the locket closer, examining it. Using her nails to open the clasp, she cries out, "Why, it's a tiny painting of an angel."

"Yes, it's called a miniature," Rouena says. She takes the necklace and places it over Sofia's head. "It's one of Maddelena's paintings."

"Maddelena was, in my humble opinion, the most talented painter in the entire medieval world," Professor Guillaume says.

"Really? I never heard of her," Mallory says.

"That's because Maddelena was never acknowledged," Rouena says. "Women were not allowed to do certain things in our time, nor could they take credit where credit was due."

"Sofia, do you understand what this is?" Professor Guillaume asks.

Sofia wraps her hand around the locket, squeezing it. "My bequest?" she asks.

"Yes," the professor says. "You are receiving it for finding Sweyn, a feat we have not been able to achieve ourselves."

"And Nash, too," Davon says. "Sofia found Nash."

"And Nash, too," Professor Guillaume repeats.

"So this locket will be of help somehow, like the other bequests?" Sofia asks.

"It is hoped," Rouena responds. The other instructors nod.

"May I ask a question?"

I grin. Could Sofia and Mallory be more opposite?

"Where is Maddelena? I mean, shouldn't she be giving this to me?"

"She should," Rouena answers, "but she knew you deserved to have it now because you will need it for the task ahead."

The task ahead? What does that mean? I feel a little sorry for myself again. With Sofia's locket, everyone has received a bequest, everyone who is still at HALO, that is. Besides, didn't I have the dream about Nash? Shouldn't someone tell me dreaming is my talent? Shouldn't I have received my bequest?

"I'm sure you are feeling left out," Rouena says in her disconcerting mind-reading way, stepping over to put her arm around my shoulder. "But all things must come in their own time."

"Speaking of time," Lionel says, rolling forward into view. "It is time for us to consider the reality of another mission." He pulls his hands off the wheels of his chair and places them in his lap.

Karl curses under his breath, and I feel my heart sink to the bottom of my feet.

"I am sorry that we did not foresee this," Lionel continues. "The possibility that you would have to go to earth as fledglings did not occur to us when we prepared to bring you here." He pauses. "Especially not twice. If we could, we would have brought you here earlier, when we were younger." He pinches the bridge of his nose. "Unfortunately, you were not born, yet."

"Lionel's right," Rouena says. "We know that we have not prepared you nearly enough. And this time you will be placed directly in the path of HALO's greatest enemy. But, you see, you must be the ones to go to earth once more. You must rescue Nash and Sweyn."

Chapter 28
Highlights

We have to wait for Maddelena to get back from the other angel communities before we can hold the planning meeting. In the meantime, I stress out over what kind of plan would work inside a demon general's domain. We'll have to use every single skill we've learned and every single bequest we've received, that's for sure.

I bring up the whole bequest topic in the great room, where, as usual, we're hanging out. "I think it's cool how each bequest fits the person it's for—armor for the warrior, a musical instrument for the musician, a medicine bag for the healer, a book for the literary genius, and a painting for the artist."

Sofia stands by the counter in the kitchen, fingering her new locket. "What do you think your bequest will be, Finn?" she asks.

"I have no idea. The only thing I've done is

dream about Nash."

How about a magic pillowcase? I could put it over my head and—what?

"You have the fleur-de-lis," Valeria says. "I know it's not your bequest, but it could be useful."

"True, but we can only use it once," Karl says.

"I think being able to put yourself into someone else's shoes is masterful," Mallory says.

"Thanks, Mallory," I say. It's rare for Mallory to compliment someone, and I guess I should be honored.

"I can't even describe how I feel about this poem. Getting this is beyond anything I could have ever imagined." The *Beowulf* manuscript is on her lap, and she runs her hands over the worn pages. "I'm not sure what I'm supposed to do with it, though, Finn, so I'm sort of in the same spot you are, aren't I? I guess I'll keep on reading it all the way through. I feel like every time I understand more of the old English."

"Sounds like fun," I say. "*Not.*" I watch as Mallory opens to the first page and her lips begin to move.

"Hey, Finn, can you help me?" Davon asks. "I thought I'd see how tough the hauberk is."

That's more up my alley. We head for the kitchen, where we open drawers and cupboard doors behind the counter, making a ton of noise as we look for sharp stuff to jab into the hauberk.

"I'm going to study Maddelena's miniature some more," Sofia says. "I might paint some, too. I'll be in my studio."

Valeria settles into the couch, reading one of Avicenne's medical books. Karl takes a break from the piano. He's pitching Riley's bone into one corner of the room after another.

Davon and I lay the hauberk over a stool and gleefully stab at it with knives, scissors, and the now useless cooking utensils. Mallory is mumbling away, when suddenly she speaks out loud. "'...*there harps rang out, clear song of the singer.*'" She lifts a page, ready to turn it.

"What was that?" Karl asks, holding Riley's rubber dog bone in mid-throw. He must have good hearing, because I didn't hear a thing.

"What was what?" I ask.

"That strumming sound," he says. "Wait. There it is again."

This time I hear it, too. It is the sound of someone's fingers running up and down harp strings. It stops abruptly. Far in the deep recesses of my brain, a thought begins to form. "Mallory," I say. "Read that line again."

"Oh, I'm sorry. I didn't realize I was reading out loud," Mallory says.

"No. It's okay. Read the one about the harps again," I say.

"Sure. '...*there harps rang out, clear song of the singer.*'" Immediately, the harp chords play again, up and down, up and down, this time louder than before.

My thought becomes a realization. "Whoa," I say. I stride over to Mallory's seat and stand in front of her. "One more time."

She peeks over the manuscript and gives me a funny look. "Gee, Finn. What are you on about?" then she reads the same line. Once more the clear, ethereal sound of a harp echoes through the room.

"Try something else," I demand.

"Okay, okay. But don't be such a git, will you?" She turns the manuscript around. "How about this one?

204

It's the next one highlighted. See?"

"Highlighted? I don't see any highlighting."

"Right there, Finn. Are you blind? It's bright orange."

"Whatever, Mallory. If anything's highlighted; you're the only one who can see it. Could you read the next highlighted one, please?"

"'*Time had now flown...*'"

`' ' ' ' ' ' '`

"...Finn? Why are you all sitting in the dark?" Sofia asks.

"What?" I turn toward her voice. It *is* dark. I peer around the room. I'm standing in front of Mallory, Valeria is still curled up on the couch with Avicenne's book, Karl and Riley are playing fetch with Riley's rubber bone, and Davon is going psycho with the knives.

"What? Is there an eclipse or something?" I ask.

"How did it get dark so fast?" Valeria asks.

"So fast," Sofia says. "I left you all— like two hours ago."

I turn back to the couch. "Mallory was reading from the manuscript," I say. A wave of excitement rolls over me. "You know what? Don't read anything else until I say so, Mallory."

"Okay," Mallory says, bewildered.

"Sofia. Everyone. Get this," I say, waving them over to the couch. "When Mallory read about the harps, we heard harps. Am I right, Karl?" Karl nods.

"When she read about time going by, well, here we are." I pause. "Let me see that manuscript, Mallory." I drop down next to her. "Show me another highlighted part."

"Um, here," she says, pointing, "and here."

"I can't see it," I say. "But Mallory, I think this is it. You know, how you're supposed to use the poem." My mind is going a mile a minute. "And I think I know how to use it, too, I mean, how you can use it to help us on our mission. It's the last piece of the puzzle."

"Puzzle?" Davon asks.

"What puzzle?" Karl asks.

I smack my forehead. "Everybody meet me back here in an hour. And make sure you have your bequests with you. I need to see Claude first, but I'm pretty sure I've come up with a rescue plan."

Chapter 29
The Calm before the Storm

Maddelena has returned. She is in Council Cottage, and for the first time since we learned the story about how the instructors formed HALO, they are all together, except Sweyn. It's hard to imagine that Maddelena could be even more beautiful than I remember, but she is. Maybe it's because she is the only angel we have never seen in her human form.

"You have no idea how overjoyed I am with the news that both Nash and Sweyn have been located," she says, and I hear her voice both aloud and in my mind. It hums with energy.

"Yes, and we must come up with the rescue plan," Professor Guillaume says.

Theo can't keep his excitement from showing. He loves this stuff. "I've got some materials with me. I believe we should begin with what we already know. The location of the warehouse—"

"Theo," Maddelena interrupts, her wings fanning wood scent over us. "You are a magnificent tactical coordinator, but there is no need for you to plan anything."

"What? Why not?" Theo asks, astonished.

"The fledglings have already come up with a plan."

Theo's mouth and mine drop open at the same time. How did Maddelena know? Avicenne's infectious laugh rings out, and out of the corner of my eye, I see the professor smile and shake his head.

"In fact, they even have a back-up plan, don't you, Finn?"

It shouldn't surprise me that Maddelena knows what we have been doing in the dormitory great room this evening. She floats over and places her hands on my shoulders, the same way she did the last time I saw her. I feel the force of her incredible power rush through my body. "Finn," she says. "You know, don't you?"

I nod. I know I have to lead this mission, or it won't work. "Each fledgling has a job to do," I say. "Mine is to tell them when to do it." I want to appear confident to Maddelena, but my palms are sweaty and my heart is pounding.

"The very definition of leadership," Maddelena remarks. She closes her mouth, but continues to speak to me with her mind. "Finn, what I meant was, do you know your talent?"

"Dreaming?" I reply, surprising myself with an ability I didn't know I had. I am speaking back to Maddelena with *my* mind.

"Finn, those are not simply dreams. You are an Empath, the most powerful of all the team. You are able to understand what another is feeling. You alone will be the last link between a human's desire to do good and his temptation to do evil."

"Finn came up with the plans," Sofia says, bringing me back to the room. There is pride in her voice, and I feel my face redden. But I realize she couldn't hear what Maddelena told me, and when I look around, I realize no one else could either. What Maddelena told me about my talent was only for my ears.

"We're going to need everyone's help here at HALO, too," I say, putting my leadership skills to work immediately. "I already asked Claude to move us to New York. We should be there any second. And Theo, we'll need a blueprint of Jarray's building, both the upstairs auction house and the downstairs warehouse."

"It's a longshot, but I think I can get one for you," Theo replies. He looks at me for a long moment before he races away.

"I will leave you to it, then," Maddelena says. "As you know, I cannot stay away from my duties for long."

I feel bad for Maddelena. As the only HALO angel who can leave the grounds, she must be overwhelmed with work.

"I have only one word of advice for the group before I go," Maddelena says. "*Speed.* You must stay in Jarray's dominion only long enough to retrieve Nash and Sweyn. General Jarray is powerful and devious, and he harbors a special hatred of HALO because of our unique ability to identify his demons. If he finds out you are in his warehouse, he will waste no time trying to put an end to your future."

Rouena can't hide the look of terror that flits across her face. "If he captured all of them—"

"Yes, Rouena, humanity would eventually perish." Maddelena's wings fan out with a razor sharp buzz, and the air swirls as she disappears to the sound of trumpets.

Theo returns with a blueprint. "It's the closest I can come, Finn, my boy." He spreads it on the round table among the fledglings' bequests.

"Okay, thanks. Everyone—why don't you sit," I say. I stand near the trunk and the painting, and explain both of the rescue plans, pointing out each relevant item we might use as I speak.

I try not to let anyone know how petrified I am, but I know the success or the failure of this mission depends on me, the only one of us fledglings who truly understands how important each individual talent is, how crucial each bequest is to the success of our mission. If even one small part of the plan goes awry, I have only one backup, and if that doesn't work, we will be unable to carry out the mission.

I also know something else my fellow fledglings don't. The true mission here is not to bring back *both* Sweyn and Nash. If we get Sweyn, that's a bonus, but *Nash* is the one we have to retrieve. If we don't bring Nash back, our group will never function the way it's supposed to. We need all seven of us, or we'll never be powerful enough to identify demons for the angel world. Without Nash, *HALO will fall apart.*

Because I am the Empath, I am the only one who can envision what the future team of HALO angels is supposed to be, and I know HALO hasn't been functioning that way since Sweyn was kidnapped over seventy years ago. Like it or not, it's up to me to

210

make sure this changes with the new team.

A heavy thud tells me we've landed in the spot outside New York City where we will make our mission preparations. I set my shoulders, take a deep breath, and let it out slowly. HALO angel community is an endangered species, and we are its only hope. It's a heavy burden for one fledgling to carry, but for now, I must carry it alone.

Kip Taylor

Day 7

It is a fact that in the right formation, the lifting power of many wings can achieve twice the distance of any bird flying alone.

-Author unknown

Kip Taylor

Chapter 30
J.R. Antiquities

We hurtle through space and land with a loud thud in the cargo hold of a freighter bound from London to New Jersey. In the cramped confines of the Trunk of Kings, the six of us, who are shielded into its contents, slam into one another.

"Ouch," Mallory cries. "You've got bloody pointed sticks for elbows, Davon."

"Can't help it," Davon replies. "Got 'em from my Momma."

"*Shush*—" I hiss. "I hear something. Be quiet."

The sound comes from a distance. Static and a gruff voice. "This is the bridge." *Squawk*. "Captain Spaulding. Ten minutes to dock at Port Newark." *Squawk*. "Tell the supercargo to have the paperwork ready to export the deadweight. Over." *Squawk*.

A louder voice, close by. "Supercargo ready, Sir." *Click*. "Over."

The gruff voice again. "Acknowledged."

Squawk. "Over and out."

The interior of our sardine can rocks to and fro as we wait out the next ten minutes, until several thumps tell me we've probably docked. Doors bang, wheels screech, men curse, and something scrapes the bottom of the packing crate, lifting us into the air with a mechanical yank.

The trunk rolls, my teeth rattle, and we come to rest at an angle. Karl's feet jam into my neck, and my head wedges awkwardly into one of the trunk's corners.

The trunk lurches, and we're rolled again, landing with a sickening crunch. I hope it means we've been loaded into a truck and the truck is headed for a certain warehouse in Manhattan. It is my intent to deliver a different cargo than Jarray expects.

An engine starts, and we rattle along.

"Do you think you could extract your knee from my nose, Finn?" Mallory asks.

"Why, certainly, Mallory," I say with exaggerated politeness. "However, finding a place to put it may be a challenge."

"My back itches again," Valeria says. "Can someone scratch it?"

"That's not Valeria's back, it's mine," Karl says. "Who is that, anyway?"

"Oops, sorry," Davon says.

"Keep your hands to yourselves, everyone," I say, sounding like a kindergarten teacher. Sofia giggles.

A few minutes later, we grind to a halt, and the absence of the engine's vibration is a relief. I hear the back doors of the truck open. The musty smell of decaying flesh seeps into the trunk. Everyone gags.

"You're going to have to deal with it," I whisper

through clenched teeth. We all know what the smell is. Demons. At least we know we're in the right place.

The demons grunt as they lift our crate from the truck and carry it into the warehouse. Moments later, I hear someone tearing at the wooden slats.

"Well, well. What have we here?" asks a disembodied voice so terrifying I find it hard to breathe. Sofia reaches through the old hatbox where she is shielded into the antique mirror where I am shielded and squeezes my hand. "I must say, this is much finer than I thought. The pictures did not do it justice. It will sell for quite a nice price. Or maybe I will keep it for my own collection."

I shudder as I imagine Jarray's hand running along the outline of the trunk. It has to be Jarray. "Interesting lock, Foelle," Jarray says, rattling it. "What do you make of this?"

A feminine voice replies. "Looks a bit like angel work to me, darling," she says. Her voice is as harrowing as nails on a chalkboard.

"You got several nice pieces from London, Sir," says a third voice.

"Yes," Jarray says. "Is there something you need, Cree?" Impatience creeps into his voice.

"Sorry to interrupt, Sir, but Silas says he needs you in the auction room. Some of the clients have already arrived."

I hear Jarray sigh. "Very well. Come along, Foelle. We shall have to revisit our deliveries later." Their footsteps echo into silence and the disgusting odor fades.

We wait a few more minutes to be sure we are alone. "Davon, get us out of here," I say, handing him the fleur-de-lis, which he uses to pry the inside of the lock open. There is a slight scraping sound as we raise the lid, before welcome gusts of air rush in, still stinking faintly of demons. Then, like noodles stuffed in a Chinese food carton, we push the various smaller antiques where we've shielded cascade over the sides of the trunk and onto the floor. We unshield, stick the antiques back in the trunk, and shut the lid. "Stick with the plan unless I tell you otherwise," I say, as everyone scatters in different directions.

I watch Davon scout the only entrances from the auction house to the warehouse, a set of three elevators on the other side of the large room from the loading dock. He gives me the thumbs up sign, which means the elevators are unguarded. This is good news. I give him the signal to stay put.

I check on Karl, who is several yards to Davon's left, crouched behind a crate, his psaltery ready. We give each other a nod.

I make sure Mallory and Sofia are in position, and I pick up Valeria, who has checked the bay doors where we were delivered. "They were locked, Finn, and there were no guards," Valeria whispers as we tiptoe toward the very darkest, deepest part of the warehouse.

The auction taking place upstairs is an important part of the plan. We want the auction to keep the demons busy so they won't be able to check the warehouse any time soon.

But we will need to heed Maddelena's warning. *Speed. Speed. Speed.* It plays in my mind, over and over, like a mantra.

Chapter 31
Alternate Uses

Valeria and I are feeling our way down a dark passageway lined with stacked boxes and antique furniture, when I see a familiar iron cell. The slats are narrow, like they were in Sofia's painting, but through them, there's a faint glow. It's Sweyn, sleeping on a pile of drop cloths.

Claude and Riley should be nearby. I whistle softly. Sure enough, Riley trots over from behind a huge bookcase.

"Good boy," I say. Riley wears his vest, his wings resting along its sides. He sits in front of me, patiently awaiting further instructions.

"Is Claude back there, boy?" I ask. Claude is our exit strategy. He has moved the school again, this time to a nearby street, and once we get what we came for, we are going to follow him out of the bay doors.

"I'm here," Claude says, emerging from the

219

darkness. He wears his usual dark suit, but he's also wearing a dark shirt, dark tie, and sunglasses. I clamp my lips shut to keep from laughing. He's definitely watched too many spy movies.

"All clear," I say. "Valeria checked."

"Then I will go finish my work," Claude says. As he turns to go, he gazes past me. "Is that who I think it is?" he asks.

"Yep," I say.

"Never thought I'd have the pleasure." Claude scurries off, and I hear a faint, "I hoped, but I certainly never thought I'd get to see Sweyn."

I grin before focusing my attention back to the iron cell. "Sweyn," I whisper. No response. "Sweyn," I repeat, using my normal voice. He stirs.

"Let me try," Valeria says. She picks up a wrench from a work bench a few yards away and bangs it lightly on the iron. I cringe. I know we're taking a chance of being heard, but Sweyn only twitches. Valeria runs the wrench across several of the iron bars. The clanging echoes.

"Okay, Valeria," I whisper nervously, "that's not going to work. We'll have to think of something else."

Valeria drops the tool. "Theo is right," she remarks. "I can see that he is unwell."

A continuous tapping noise interrupts us. It is not one of the signals we have all agreed upon. "What's that?" I ask. The tapping gets louder and more insistent.

"Over there," Valeria says. "I think it's coming from behind that big stack of chairs."

"I'll check," I say. "You stay here." I creep around the corner. There, in an iron cell similar to Sweyn's, sits Nash. His arms are tied behind his back, and his mouth is covered with duct tape.

Duct tape? Demons need to use duct tape?

Nash scoots toward me and makes some frantic muffled sounds. I lift my hand to touch the bars, but he shakes his head back and forth with force.

"Don't touch the bars, Finn."

I jump ten feet in the air. "Shoot, Valeria. You scared me. I thought you were back with Sweyn."

"Sorry. I got scared." She crouches in front of Nash's iron prison cell. "Is that what you were trying to say, Nash? Don't touch the bars?" Nash nods.

I tell Valeria to go get Sofia, and while she's gone, I ask Nash a series of nod-yes or shake-your-head-no questions. When Valeria returns, Sofia in tow, I have a little more information I might need.

Sofia removes her necklace and slips her fingernail under the filigree. The locket opens with a soft pop. The side opposite the miniature painting holds a tiny key. Maddelena has informed Sofia that the key may have the power to open the cell door.

Except we can't seem to find a door. Sofia, Valeria, and I search high and low without touching any bars, but there is no obvious door. Then I remember Riley. "Hey, boy," I say. "Find the door for us, okay?"

Riley dashes to the far side of the iron pen. He runs along the length of it and sniffs out a spot midway between the top and the bottom.

"Great job, boy," I say. "Here, Sof. Give the key to me." I'm afraid she will get a shock like the one I got from HALO's door.

"No, Finn," Sofia says. "This is my job. I will use the power of the locket and the key."

Though it makes sense, I'm still worried.

Sofia pokes the key carefully around the place

221

where Riley sits. After a few moments, the key disappears and a portion of the cell opens inwards. I crawl in, careful not to touch the bars on either side, and tear the tape from Nash's mouth.

"Ouch," he says.

"Ouch? We come into demon territory to save your life, and all you have to say is 'ouch?'"

"It hurt," Nash whines. He ducks his head and peers around me. "Hey, Sof. Hey, Val."

"It's good to see you," Sofia says.

"Oh, Nash," Valeria says. "Why do you do these things?"

"We don't have time for idle chit-chat," I say, incredulous at how casual they're all acting. "We need to get out of here. We're in a demon's warehouse, remember? The auction could be over any minute."

Speed. Speed. Speed.

"Can you get these off me?" Nash asks. He twists to one side so I can see his hands, bound together with some kind of rope made out of red metal.

"I've never seen that before. It's probably some kind of demon technology. We don't have time to mess around with it right now."

Nash glares at me.

"Sorry," I say, but I only half mean it. "Listen, Nash. I promise we'll get them off as soon as we can." I crawl backwards out of the cell, and Nash follows on his knees. By the time he's out, he's breathing heavily.

"Girls," Nash says, gazing up at them. "You are a sight for sore eyes." Each of the girls hooks an arm through one of Nash's elbows, and as they haul him to his feet, he groans.

"What's wrong?" Valeria asks. She lets go of Nash's arm, and for the first time, I notice his burns, large raw patches of skin in various stages of healing.

Nash shrugs. "Nothing you can't help me with, Valeria, my favorite healer-angel-chick," he says, grinning.

"C'mon, Nash. Cut it out. We have to wake up Sweyn," I say. I start to walk away, disgusted with Nash's attitude. Doesn't he have a clue what we're all risking?

I gaze back. "Sofia, go get Karl, okay?" For a moment, I let myself wish the two of us could be alone together, anywhere but here. "And, Sof? Can I borrow that key?"

She locks eyes with me, raises one eyebrow, and hands over the key. My mood darkens even further as I lose sight of her.

"So, who are we waking up?" Nash asks.

"Later," I hiss. I'm not about to explain anything to him right now. I rush ahead. When I reach Sweyn's cage, I ask Riley to find the door, and I open the lock with Sofia's necklace key. Valeria arrives with Nash, and we put him in an armchair to wait.

I run a continuous conversation with my dad in my mind to calm me down. *How am I doing so far?* I ask. *Fine, son,* he replies, *but, there's always a calm before the storm.*

I hear someone approaching, and a huge shadow appears behind us. I break out in a cold sweat. my heart leaps, and I get ready to fight or flee. It's Karl, his size thirteens slapping on the concrete floor. "Boy, am I glad it's you," I say. I close my eyes and talk to my dad again. Then I tell Karl, "Time to do your thing."

Sofia trots up, and she and Valeria pull a bench over for Karl. He sits, puts the psaltery on his lap, and makes a few adjustments before he begins to play.

223

"I sure hope this back up plan works," I say in a loud whisper. Then I go inside the cell and crouch before the long lost angel of the first HALO team.

As Karl plays, I see the colors flowing out of the psaltery, exactly like they did when we were in Lionel's tapestry. They bend and stretch across the space toward Sweyn and me, and then they wrap around Sweyn's head. Will they be able to penetrate the demon stupor? If not, we may have to try to carry Sweyn back, and that will be hard, maybe impossible.

Sweyn's eyes blink. Then his fingers quiver, and the motion travels through his arms and legs until his entire body shakes. He brings his hands up to his face and rubs his eyes. I lean closer, and as his eyes open, a radiant smile breaks across his handsome face. "Am I dreaming?" he asks. "No, that's impossible. I have had only nightmares these past years. How many years, I wonder."

"I'm Finn," I say, as Valeria rushes into the cell. She opens her bag, takes out the bottle containing the medicine of the four temperaments, and unscrews the cap. "You've been here for over seventy years."

"Ah, the *healer*," Sweyn says, turning his attention to Valeria.

"Just a drop," Valeria says. She touches the glass stopper to Sweyn's lips. "We must do this slowly." Valeria is entranced, unable to look away from Sweyn.

"Yes," Sweyn says. "Thank you. This will help me walk. But a warning, I will be unable to fly for quite some time."

"That's okay," I say. "We can't fly either."

Sweyn's eyes open wide. "You haven't gotten your wings yet?" he asks. "It couldn't be. You're not still fledglings, are you?" He gives Valeria and me the once over. Then he seems to notice Karl, Sofia and Nash outside of the cell. "Are all the others with you?"

"Yes," I say. "All seven of us and an assistant angel named Claude. And Riley, my dog. It's a long story."

Sweyn throws his head back and howls with laughter. It's even more appealing than Avicenne's laugh. "A long story, eh? Yes, I can imagine that it is."

"So, if you're feeling up to walking, we should get going. We're kind of in a time crunch, here," I say.

Sweyn laughs again. "The best idea I have heard in—what did you say? Over seventy years? Let's get out of here, then, shall we, Finn?" Sweyn reaches his hand out to me, and I grab it with both of mine and pull him up.

Karl stows the psaltery, and he and Sofia help Nash to his feet. Valeria and I each take one of Sweyn's arms, and lead him out of the cell. It's time for us to leave the warehouse.

I fear this part of our plan the most, especially since everything has been going fairly well so far. We'll meet Mallory and Davon at the loading bay, where Claude will be waiting for us with one of the garage doors unlocked.

Of course, everything depends on the auction continuing upstairs.

Chapter 32
Strength of Evil

"How is my Maddelena?" Sweyn asks, as we shuffle toward the bay doors at the back of the warehouse. I feel like we're dragging him. Valeria and Karl are a few steps in front of us. Everyone is moving in slow motion, and my mind is screaming.

Speed. Speed. Speed.

"She is beautiful," Sofia tells Sweyn. "The most beautiful angel I have ever seen."

"She saved my life," I say, trying not to pull Sweyn's arm out of its socket.

"I expected she might have to do that for one of you," Sweyn says. He shakes his head from side to side. "Imagine. Fledglings. And *you* are saving *me*." He clears his throat. "'...*The catapult which seeks the fortress strong, It is for you to find what must be done...*,'" he says.

My stomach lurches as another line from the sonnet pops into my head, and I think it's a good thing

I don't eat anymore. "'*Yet evil hath a way of gaining strength…*,'" I say.

Sweyn looks at me in surprise, sending a message from his mind to mine. Panic grips me. "We have to get out of here, right now, don't we?"

"Yes," he replies. "It would appear so."

We reach the back of the warehouse. Claude waits in front of the partially open garage door. It is night, and the lights of New York City blink in the distance.

I let go of Sweyn's arm, and he and Valeria duck their heads under the door. Karl, Nash, and Sofia follow. I watch Sofia, breathing a sigh of relief as she goes out, but then she lets go of Nash's arm and steps back inside. I wave her off. "Sofia, it's not safe."

She nods, begins to turn back, and suddenly a long black whip comes out of nowhere, wraps around her waist, and drags her, shrieking, into the warehouse.

My heart plummets. "Go," I scream to Valeria and Karl. "Take care of them. I'm counting on you."

Karl drops Nash's arm, and his eyes meet mine. I can tell he questions whether or not he should leave.

"Wait," Sweyn says, as Valeria pulls him toward the darkness. He twists a large gold signet ring, pulling it from his left index finger. When it comes off, he motions me to him, grasps my left hand, and slides the ring on my index finger. "You will need this." He and Valeria fade into the darkness, Karl hauls Nash off the loading bay, and they vanish, too.

I try desperately to pull my thoughts together. Mallory and Davon are missing. I hope they are not in trouble. "Claude," I say, turning to the guardian angel waiting by the door. "No matter what happens, don't wait any longer than five minutes. Then, take Riley and lead the others back to HALO as planned."

I don't wait for him to answer. Instead, I sprint into the warehouse, because without Sofia I don't want to be a HALO angel. I don't want to be anything.

The black whip was a snake. As I get near the elevators, the entire floor is covered with them. They're climbing the packing crates and the furniture, jutting out like moving sticks into the narrow aisles, writhing and hissing. I duck under them, hop over them, and stomp as many as I can, but more are pouring out from under the elevator doors like rushing water.

To my dismay, Davon and Mallory are still at their posts, overwhelmed by snakes, helplessly striking them away. "We got caught," Mallory cries.

"Where is Sofia?" I yell. I will have to get them together if I have the slightest chance of saving them.

Mallory points to the farthest elevator. "There."

I kick more snakes away, heading in the direction Mallory pointed. From the corner of my eye, I see Mallory struggle with her copy of *Beowulf*. She flings the leather satchel at the snakes and thumbs through the manuscript.

"Arrrrgh, I can't find the bloody page," she wails.

I reach Sofia, who has wedged herself between the elevator and a vending machine. She darts out, flings both arms around my neck, and jumps into my arms. I tell myself I'm never going to let her go.

"You don't need the page," I call out, dancing among the snakes as I carry Sofia toward Mallory and Davon. "You've memorized it." I'm surprised to hear how calm my voice sounds.

"I forget," Mallory screams. She gazes at the ceiling, dropping the book to the floor.

"C'mon, Mallory," I say. "That's something Nash would say. You never forget anything."

Mallory's mouth drops open, she rams her glasses up her nose, and then she yells, "'*Then sank they to sleep.*'"

Thuds. Thousands of thuds. The snakes collapse to the ground, unconscious.

Sofia hugs me so hard I fear she'll break my neck. "Oh, Finn," she says, hysterical, "you know how I hate snakes."

"I'm here, Sofia," I croak. "Mallory took care of it. You're okay, now. You're okay." I set Sofia down, and with Davon and Mallory just behind us, lead the way back to the loading bay, stepping carefully over the sleeping snakes. I glance back once. Mallory is shoving the manuscript back into its leather case. Davon is walking backward to keep an eye out.

Claude is still standing by the door like a faithful dog, and the real dog is barking like crazy.

"Quiet, Riley," I say. "You'll give us away." I nudge Sofia and Mallory out the bay doors. They know where to go. It has been prearranged.

Sofia clutches my arm. "I'm not leaving you here," she says.

"But we're coming right away, aren't we Claude?" I remove her hand and gesture for Mallory to take it. "It's okay, Sof." Mallory and Sofia fade into the black night, and I hear them murmuring. Davon follows.

"Now, Claude," I say, when I am sure they are out of danger, "We just have to close the door. It'll give us more time to get away."

"Oh, I don't think it will, really," a voice behind me says.

I whirl around, squinting into the darkness. I know whose voice it is. Jarray steps out of the shadows. I understand how he could be handsome and appealing to humans. His head is shaved, his body is what my football coach would call "a perfect physical specimen," and he wears expensive, elegant clothing from head to toe. But his foul odor and blood-red aura is an abomination to me.

"Foelle, do you think closing the bay door would have given this fledgling and his little angel friend more time?" he asks.

"Of course not, darling," Foelle agrees.

I know she is as powerful as Jarray, and considered a perfect specimen also. Humans would think her beautiful in a Gothic, dark way, but she smells even worse than Jarray, and underneath her magenta aura, I see the shape-shifting monsters within her.

"I would have smelled them anywhere," Foelle says, in a gurgling voice. "It's that sickening sweet smell of flowers and rain and goodness. It always makes me want to puke."

I have no backup plan for this.

"I know how you got in, of course," Jarray says. "I had a feeling about that trunk, didn't I, Foelle?"

"You and I should have opened it then," Foelle says. "I could have used a few tasty hors d'oeuvres before the auction." She cackles like a witch.

"Very clever of you, fledglings," Jarray continues. "Waiting until I am busy with the auction, figuring out how to open the cages, even putting my little soldiers to sleep."

I feel Claude more than I see him. He rushes past me, tackling Jarray at his knees and knocking him to the floor. Riley bounds after Claude, and I almost don't recognize my sweet little dog, viciously biting at Jarray's neck. "I don't like you," Claude cries, as he pounds on Jarray with his fists. "I certainly do not like you. *I—have—never—liked—you!*"

Beside them, Foelle metamorphoses into a raging, frothing fiend, turning her wrath on me. This scene is familiar, and for a moment, I relive my kidnapping. It brings me a strength I didn't know I had. We're about to collide, when Davon steps in front of me. Foelle spews vile liquid into his chest, but it bounces off the hauberk like a rubber ball.

I thought Davon was with Sofia.

Jarray grabs Riley by the scruff. He throws him off, and Riley turns, barking furiously. Then Jarray wraps his hands around Claude's neck, and like he's throwing away a piece of trash, tosses him to Foelle. Foelle melts, covering Claude with slime.

The ring Sweyn just put on my finger begins to hum. I rush by Davon and raise my left hand. The vibration increases, and white flame shoots out, striking the center of the slime pile. An electric pulse ripples out in wide waves. The slime explodes, pieces flying off into the warehouse and evaporating into thin air.

Jarray stares in shock at the spot where the explosion took place, and I jump at the chance to escape. Curling my arm around Davon, I haul him out with me to the loading dock. We tear down the alley, my legs pumping automatically. A blur that is Riley flies past. Behind us, I hear Jarray's curses and wails floating in the air.

We slow to a fast walk, and I can't get away from the images in my mind. At the moment, I'm sorry I have the gift I do. I can see Jarray, clear as day. He sits on the floor, his head in his hands. Curled nearby is the tiny body of Claude, his once impeccable suit covered in what's left of the slime that was Foelle, his face burned beyond recognition.

Chapter 33
Finding the Way

My tears blind me, so I concentrate on Riley, prancing just ahead. Out of breath, every muscle aching, Davon and I reach the end of the alley, stop for a moment, and then clutching each other, turn left onto a busy New York City street. Here, we find everyone clustered under the awning of the restaurant where we arranged to meet. Well-dressed couples, some carrying packages from the auction at J.R. Antiquities, wait in line to enter the restaurant.

"There they are," Sofia cries, as Davon and I hobble toward the group.

Neither Davon nor I can speak.

"Finn, what's wrong? Why are you so upset? Where's Claude?" Sofia asks. She envelops me in her arms and pulls me a few feet away. Valeria and Mallory follow us.

"Claude didn't make it," I say. "Foelle got him."

Sofia takes her sleeve and wipes my face.

"Oh," Valeria says, putting her hand up to her mouth. Tears run down her cheeks.

"But how are we going to get back to HALO without Claude?" Mallory asks.

I shake my head. I have no idea. "Foelle is gone, too, if that's any consolation," I say. "At least there's some good news."

"Yes, that is good news," Sofia says. "What about Jarray?"

"He'll be coming after us soon," I say.

"Then we'll have to pull ourselves together and do this without Claude."

"You're right," I say, straining to focus on the rest of the mission. "We'll have to find HALO by ourselves."

Sofia puts her arm around my waist and leans her head against my shoulder. "It will be all right, Finn. I have a feeling Claude has gone straight to the Light."

"We probably shouldn't stay here very long," Mallory says, being practical. "It's awfully close to the auction house."

I agree. We trudge back to the restaurant where I briefly update the rest of the group with the news of both Claude's and Foelle's deaths.

"And since Claude was the part of our plan that involved finding our way back," I say, "it falls to us to find HALO now. The building has to be here somewhere. It will look like the others, but there will be something about it that we should recognize."

Nash has pulled a tourist map out of a kiosk near the restaurant. He has it spread open in front of him, and he's scanning it intently. I open my mouth to ask for suggestions, but I don't even get a word out before Nash has one.

"We'll have to spread out in four directions," he says. "I'm guessing we are about three or four blocks from the school. Finn, you and Sofia stay here with Sweyn. He's still vulnerable. Maybe go inside the restaurant. It could be good cover."

Rouena's voice echoes in my head. *He has the gift of solving problems.*

"Karl, you go north to 52nd St., then west. Davon, you're south on 10th Ave. Mallory and Valeria, stick together and go north on 10th Ave. I'll go east, back down the alley. We'll meet back here in ten minutes."

"The instructors should be looking out for us," I say. "But hurry. We don't have much time."

Karl, Davon, and the girls take off running. Riley dashes after Karl.

"Nash, I better go with you if you're headed back toward the warehouse," I say. "Sofia can stay with Sweyn by herself, right Sof?"

Sofia nods and grips Sweyn tightly. "Of course," she says.

"Okay," Nash agrees. "Let's go, then."

Nash and I hustle toward the alley in back of the antique warehouse. My stomach churns as we pass the loading bay, but I notice the lights are off and the bay door is down. We pick up our pace, continuing to 9th Ave.

"Should we go north to 52nd like you told Karl, or south to 51st?" I ask. "We're leaving unexplored territory either way."

"We could split up. Meet me back in two."

"Okay." I sprint south to 51st and cut over to 8th Ave. To keep from going insane, I sing show tunes, the words sputtering as my breath becomes more ragged. I think it's a good thing no human being can see or hear me. In the end, I find nothing out of the ordinary, and I arrive at the meeting spot before Nash. When he trots up, we head back.

Everyone huddles in front of the restaurant again, except Karl. No one has found HALO. Then we see Karl's tall form round the corner of 52nd St. He has a big smile on his face. Riley bolts ahead of him. I kneel, and Riley runs into my arms.

"Good boy," I say. "Did you guys find it?"

"Riley found it," Karl says, out of breath and laughing. "I guess we forgot he came with Claude. Anyway, it's this way. C'mon." He motions us across the street, and I scoop up Riley, who puts his paws over my shoulders.

"I almost missed it," Karl says. "It's a hotel. But then I saw revolving doors. I remembered them from before, in San Diego. Riley was barking like crazy, so I looked closer, and there was Rouena inside, signaling to me. They're waiting for us."

We jog down 52nd St. Sweyn is limping, falling behind, when he stops abruptly. I figure he's going to tell us we have to help him more, but he jerks his head back in the direction of the antique warehouse. "I hear Jarray," Sweyn says. "Listen."

Over the normal sounds of Manhattan, I think I hear sounds of crackling fire and shrieking animals. *"Run faster,"* I yell.

The roar gets louder just as I see the revolving doors and a sign for **Hotel One**, *New York's Most Historic Hotel.* I tap Valeria's shoulder. "Go two at a time," I say. "You and Mallory first." I drop Riley in with them, and all three disappear. The door turns faster as Sofia and Sweyn follow, then Karl and Davon, and last, Nash and me.

Nash and I are halfway in when the buzzing roar of insects and the powerful stench of demon reach us. A black talon snags my arm, and I feel it rip the skin from the top of my forearm to my wrist. "Nash," I scream. "*Help!*"

Nash yanks my arm, now stuck in the door, and hauls me the rest of the way into the moving triangle. With a last burst of energy, we push the door and collapse into the lobby of the nonexistent hotel.

We're safe.

I lay there, gazing at the black and white floor tiles, unable to move. I hear a faint tinkling sound, like a fountain, and I smell sweet flowers and rain and goodness.

Chapter 34
A Resplendent Reunion

We talk and hug and most of us shed at least a few tears. Lionel leaves to take over Claude's job, moving us out of New York as quickly as possible. The rest of us make our way up the stairs and crowd into Welcome Cottage.

The instructors can't take their eyes off Sweyn. They ask him questions non-stop, while Avicenne tends to his legs. She soon has him almost able to walk without a limp. Still, he is not himself. His wings are at half-mast, and his aura is faint and grayish. Valeria stays busy, too, tending to Nash's burns and my gaping talon wound.

"Tell us what happened to Claude," Theo says.

"Let me tell," Davon says. He gets up to stand by the fire, and his eyes glisten with tears as he describes the attack by Foelle in vivid detail. "He was so brave," Davon says. "He gave his life to save Finn's and mine, just like a real hero." Theo's head bobs up and down as Davon speaks. I know these are the kind of stories he lives for.

"Here, here," I say, softly.

Then, to my embarrassment, Davon brings up my name. "Finn got Foelle, though," Davon says. "He zapped her with that ring of yours, Sweyn."

Sweyn smiles broadly. "It's your bequest, Finn," he says.

I gaze at Rouena. She is smiling, too.

"Yes, Finn. It was never here for you to receive."

Theo's been examining Nash's handcuffs. "I think I have something that will get those off," he says. He takes Nash outside, and they return within moments, the red handcuffs gone, both of them grinning.

"What did you do?" Karl asks.

"Oh, just something you haven't learned about yet," Theo says. "There is quite of bit of that, you know."

Mallory and Valeria are still upset about Claude, and Rouena is deep in conversation with them. "But was he close enough to his time?" I hear Mallory ask.

"No, but Maddelena intervened," Rouena replies.

"I'll let Sofia know," Valeria says. "She had a feeling."

I remember what Sofia said about Claude going to the Light. I never saw Maddelena at the warehouse, but if she arrived in time, saving Claude's life force and taking him to the Light would have been the best use of her power.

"Thank goodness Nash had the idea to split

up," Karl comments. "We would never have found this place in time if we had stuck together."

"Dude," Nash says, rubbing his wrists where the handcuffs were. "I don't deserve any credit."

"What?" Mallory asks. "Did we bring back the wrong Nash?"

"Don't get ahead of yourself, Mal-*icious*," Nash says. "But to answer your bazillionth question since we got here, no. I just had some friends come and rescue me, and I appreciate it."

The fireplace roars to life. Hundreds of candles lining the beams of the ceiling and the mantle flicker on. A cool breeze, smelling of wood, raises the hairs on the back of my neck and along my arms. I have been anticipating this moment. I elbow Sofia gently. "It's Maddelena," I whisper.

She materializes in a peal of girlish laughter, and though she looks tired, her aura is blazing pink. "Nash, I'm afraid you'll need to take a bit of credit," Maddelena says. "Without your stubborn determination to go back to earth and protect your girlfriend, Sweyn would still be missing." She eyes the rest of us. "I owe all of you, in fact. Thank you, fledglings. Thank you all so much."

Sweyn, with no sign of his former limp, vaults across the room and throws his arms around Maddelena. He speaks to her from his mind. "Maddelena, you are impossibly gorgeous, as ever. I am told I have spent over seventy years in Jarray's prison, but the true torture was every moment spent away from you."

Maddelena's pink aura sweeps over Sweyn, and light bursts forth in every color of the rainbow. Sweyn's aura turns to a glittering golden color, and his wings spread out over five feet on either side, falling all the way to the floor majestically.

They are the most magnificent creatures I have ever seen.

"Imagine," Sweyn continues. "Even we could not have foreseen how powerful the fledglings would be. My fears for our own voyage into the Light and the possible extinction of the human race have been conquered."

"Yes, my dear, dear Sweyn," Maddelena says. "Together, these fledglings can work miracles. You are evidence of that." She holds Sweyn away from her at arms' length. She scrutinizes him from top to bottom and shakes her head. "Lionel," she says, "will you begin the preparations? Let's schedule the festivities for a week from this evening." Once again she erupts in girlish musical laughter. "We have much to celebrate."

Rouena nods, and getting up, says it has been a long day, she's sure we're all exhausted, and it's time for us to go back to the dormitory and relax or sleep.

Nash falls into step with me on the way out. "I hope they're so busy getting ready for their party they have to cancel classes," he says, punching me in the arm.

Some things never change.

Kip Taylor

One Week Later

Angels are spirits, but it is not because they are spirits that they are angels. They become angels when they are sent.

-St. Augustine

Kip Taylor

Finn Flanagan and the Fledglings

Chapter 35
Leaving the Nest

Some things do change. The instructors are being super-secretive about their party, but they've shown us some great new places to hang out and do whatever we want, and every morning, Nash and I go surfing. It turns out there's a beach with great waves on the other side of the mountain. It also turns out I'm not half-bad at surfing.

Some things don't change. Classes aren't cancelled. We have a few more, and Mallory still raises her hand constantly in every one of them.

On the morning of the celebration, Valeria and Karl are kayaking, and Davon is off somewhere with Theo and Riley. Nash is playing pinball, and Mallory is lying on the couch, reading.

After wondering for a moment whether it's safe to leave Nash and Mallory alone together, I make my way to Sofia's studio, where I know I will find her. I flop back on a futon as she picks colors from the rack of tubes and squeezes some onto her palette. I've decided to tell her that I like her. A lot. "Hey, Sof," I say.

"Yeah, Finn."

I can't believe it. I chicken out. "I could sit here and watch you paint all day," I say.

I want to kick myself.

"Thanks, Finn," she replies, a smile tugging at the corners of her mouth.

I want her to set her brushes down and look at me. I know if she does, she'll be able to see how I feel, and I won't have to tell her. But, she's never going to let me off that easy. "What do you think is going to happen tonight?" I ask, for the hundredth time.

"I'm not sure. I think we're going to celebrate the return of Sweyn. Maybe they'll thank us for rescuing him," she says. "What do you think?

She knows what I think. We've had this conversation before. "Yeah, that's what I think, too."

Really, this is crazy. I'm such a coward.

Sofia sets down her palette. My heart skips a beat. "Will you scratch my back?" she says. "It itches right here." She sits on her stool, and I get up off the futon and scratch. It occurs to me that where I'm scratching her is the exact same place my back has been itching.

"That okay?" I ask.

She nods and stretches. "Yes. Thanks, Finn."

It's the perfect time. We're alone, she is right here beside me— all I have to do is open my mouth and speak. But once again, I blow my opportunity. Sofia picks up her palette and returns to her painting.

I crash back onto the futon, curse myself under

my breath, and give up. I don't deserve someone as awesome as Sofia. Finally, I fall asleep watching her long fingers dabbing and sliding her brush on the canvas.

\ \ \ \ \ \ \

At sunset, Avery opens the front door of the dorm and calls for us. "Helloooooo," he coos. "I have come to escort you to the party."

I'm out first, and tears come to my eyes as I see Avery's outfit. He's wearing a gray pinstriped suit, a crisp white shirt, and a banana-colored tie.

Karl, Davon, and Nash bound out behind me, also dressed in suits, and then the girls trickle in, one-by-one, in beautiful long gowns. Valeria is first, wearing a gauzy green strapless, Mallory second in black velvet with a large cream-colored bow at the waist. Sofia steps out last, and I gasp out loud. She's wearing a pink halter dress, and the clingy silk swirls around her perfect figure.

"You girls look fab-u-los-o," Karl says.

"You're not bad yourselves," Mallory replies.

"We know," Nash says, grinning. He offers Mallory an elbow. "Like chicken? Grab a wing." Mallory bursts out laughing.

I offer Sofia my arm, and Karl and Davon each offer one of theirs to Valeria. Avery clears his throat, swipes at his eyes, and tells us gruffly we don't want to be late. He leads us in a direction we have never been, out the front door of the dormitory and to the right, on a path that materializes between two lines of pine trees.

The trees overhang, and the walk is magical. Riley putter along behind us, his collar adorned with a bright blue bow.

When a glow appears in the dark sky, Avery quickens his pace. "We're almost there," he says. He's more excited than a little kid at a birthday party.

A few minutes later, the path opens into a space about the size and shape of a football stadium. Thousands of angels spread out along the rocky edges of the mountains. Some are resting on little carved out seats in the rock, and other float in the air. Each angel has wings, a halo, and an aura. The difference is, I notice no auras as intense as our instructors, nor do I see any other full-length wings.

Scattered among the angels are doll-like creatures about six inches tall. The distant ones look like flickering lightning bugs, but the one closer are perfect miniature angels, only their wings are shimmery-clear and their auras are tiny flames.

"The little ones are the Light Spirits," Avery says. "It is a special privilege to have them here."

All seven of our instructors sit like rock stars on a platform suspended over clouds in the middle of the stadium, and hovering over the entire scene, the sun and the moon shine together, like newly-minted coins.

Avery points us in the direction of the platform, where seven empty chairs are lined up beside the instructors' chairs. "Sit there, little birds," he says, shooing us toward the cloud field.

As soon as the crowd spots us, a riot of noise breaks out. An overwhelming blast of trumpets, plunking and strumming harp strings, flapping wings, choral singing, and the charming giggles of the Light Spirits fill the air.

We cross the field, Riley bringing up the rear, and climb the platform. We cross in front of the instructors, and as the last in line, my seat is right next to Rouena's. I nudge her as I sit. "This isn't a just a party for Sweyn, is it?" I whisper.

"No, Finn, and right now you are being applauded. Enjoy it."

I gaze around for Avery and find him in the front row, next to the Peekers. The Sergeant has a bandage wrapped around his head, and he's wearing the same World War I uniform he was wearing in Jordana's hospital room, the one that looks like he's still on the beach at Normandy. He stands and salutes, and as I salute back, Betty tugs on his jacket. "Snorty, for goodness sake, sit down. You're making a spectacle of yourself," she says. Then she smiles, waves, and goes back to fiddling with her pearls.

A few moments later, Sweyn stands, his wings shimmering and his aura like fireworks, and he hushes the crowd with outstretched arms. "Light Spirits, fellow guardian angels, and fellow members of HALO," he announces. "We find ourselves poised upon the brink of a new era."

Sweyn reaches for Maddelena's hand, pulling her up to join him. Maddelena lets her wings loose as she stands, and the glorious light they create together takes my breath away. A cacophony of sound fills the stadium. Sweyn puts his arm around Maddelena and hushes the crowd once more.

Maddelena speaks. "Tonight, all of you have the privilege of meeting the HALO fledglings. These seven young men and woman are the former humans who will soon replace us as leaders of HALO. Many of you know their parents, grandparents, and other family members from previous generations."

The crowd buzzes with excited chatter, and

Maddelena waits patiently for them to settle down.

"The fledglings have already proven themselves to be invaluable to the angel world," Maddelena continues. "To stand among you and celebrate the return of Sweyn is nothing short of a miracle."

The din becomes deafening.

Maddelena turns. "Rouena, HALO's headmistress, will now tell you about each of the candidates."

Nash leans around the back of Sofia. "This is embarrassing," he whispers. "I don't like being the center of attention."

"Yes, you do," I say.

Caught, he smiles.

Rouena introduces us one-by-one, making each of us stand while she talks. She includes a little of our pasts on earth, what our talents are, what bequest we got, and even a little about each of our personalities. It's how she ends each introduction that astounds me. Finally, we learn of the link between one of us and one of them. Why did I not see this before?

Nash is the descendant of Rouena, of course. Who else has those aqua eyes? Mallory descends from Professor Guillaume's family tree of geniuses, Valeria is one of a long line of healers in Avicenne's family, Davon is Theo's little soldier, and Lionel has passed his musical gene to Karl. I'm not surprised Maddelena is Sofia's artistic ancestor. I am proud to learn that I am the descendant of Sweyn, and since I don't know much about him yet, I look forward to finding out how we are similar. I also want to find out more about the Ring of Paladin.

Whenever Rouena pauses, the angels and Light Spirits continue to erupt, filling the stadium with music, sparkling light displays, and the unique clamor or rustling wings.

After each of us has stood in the limelight, Sweyn asks all of us to stand. He swings his arm in an arc over his head and utters something in Latin.

My back begins to itch unbearably, right between my shoulder blades, but I hardly have time for it to bother me. In a matter of seconds, the itch is gone, and I hear a series of soft *whooshes*.

Sofia almost knocks me over when a full set of shoulder-to-waist wings springs from her back. I feel the weight of my own wings pull me backwards. I peer down the line, and a motley group of proud, slightly dazed, winged angels gazes back.

Somebody places a hat on my head, and my entire body begins to tingle. But it's not a hat, it's a halo, and the tingling is my aura. My aura is gold, like Sweyn's, Sofia's a bright shade of pink, Valeria's green, Karl's purple, Mallory's yellow, Davon's orange, and Nash's a bright turquoise blue.

I try to remember the lesson when we learned what each aura color represents, and soon it comes to me. Pink is love, green is for healing, purple represents music, yellow means joy and freedom of thought, orange equals power, and blue is for force and energy. But what does gold mean? I'll have to ask Sweyn, I guess.

Sweyn stretches his arms out again, and speaks to us. "As you can see, the seven of you are no longer fledglings. You have earned an early graduation," he says. "You have been given the next rank of angel, and as such, are now true angels, with halo, wings, auras, and the power and responsibility that goes along with your rank." He pauses. "We now proclaim you guardian angels. Congratulations!" Then, raising his voice, he presents us to the crowd. "Here is the future of HALO for the next thousand years."

The burst of noise that follows is the loudest of the night. Maybe it's because it includes the seven of us "former fledglings." We scream, laugh, and jump up and down. We try to hug each other, but our new wings get in the way, so we end up high-fiving instead.

A trumpet blast, louder than even the crowd noise, brings us back. It's Lionel, blowing the largest conch shell I've ever seen. "Angels," he yells, repeating himself several times while we all get quiet. Finally, the Light Spirits stop their spins and the angel community representatives settle down in their seats.

"I'm afraid I must interrupt our celebration," Lionel says. "I have received a special report from earth." Something about Lionel's tone of voice gets my immediate full attention. "I hate to be the bearer of terrible news, especially during such a joyous and important celebration, but General Jarray has already struck a blow. He has bombed a dormitory in England, possibly killing over a hundred college students. Rumors are spreading that this is only the first of a full-scale retaliation for Jarray's partner's death. My sources tell me The Righteous is plotting catastrophic events around the world."

"Do you know any of the plans?" Maddelena asks.

"Not specifically, but other terrorist activities and natural disasters have been mentioned. Jarray is furious at the fledglings for destroying his beloved Foelle. He claims that he will destroy what we love most, too, humanity itself."

The hushed silence turns to expressions of

surprise and fear, and the stadium darkens, as one-by-one the angels and the Light Spirits leave, leaving the stands empty. We're left standing on the platform like the losing home team players whose fans have abandoned them before the game is over.

"What do you want us to do?" I ask.

"Let's get you back to the dormitory," Rouena says. "There's nothing we can do right away."

"Once again, we'll have to accelerate your lessons," Professor Guillaume says.

"First thing tomorrow, I will give you instruction in Contemplation and Rest," Avicenne says. "You will need it to replace the sleep that you no longer need."

"Yes, they will need C & R, Avi, if they are to participate in crisis planning sessions," Theo agrees. Then he adds, "And I will help you adjust to your new appendages."

"Appendages?" Valeria asks. "Oh, you mean our wings."

"How about for the rest of tonight, you enjoy each other's company," Rouena says. "Try not to worry." She's like a mother hen.

The instructors fly off over the mountain, and Avery leads us back the way we came. He keeps peeking back over his shoulder as we walk the narrow path, though it's more of a half-walk, half-float. I'm having some trouble. My wings keep lifting me when I'm not expecting it. And I'm not the only one.

When we get to the wider part of the path, near the dormitory, Nash knocks into me.

"Oops," he says, snickering. We both sail into the air, and Nash extracts his right wing from the top of my left one. Then Nash knocks into me again, and this time I realize he's doing it on purpose. I push him back, and he flies four feet or so, where he collapses into a heap.

Nash bursts out laughing and pops back up from the ground. Moments later, he dive-bombs Karl, who then rams into Davon. The girls join in, and before you know it, we're playing flying bumper cars.

I promise myself that soon I'll worry about the responsibility of fighting Jarray again. I promise myself I'll spend the next thousand years protecting humanity. But for the moment, I have confidence our instructors will teach us what we need to know, my HALO peers and I will be able to use our talents and bequests, and as a group, we will work together to accomplish whatever we are supposed to do.

Davon bashes into me, and as I soar toward the trees, I grab Sofia's hand and pull her along. She dissolves into adorable giggles, and her hair's honeysuckle scent wafts over me like a magic spell. And that's when I make one more promise to myself. I promise that someday soon, someday in the *very* near future, I will pluck up the courage to tell Sofia how I feel.

Acknowledgements

Much appreciation and thanks to:
-NaNoWriMo, for the dynamite,
-Michael Conner, for time above and beyond, for great additions of humor and creativity, and for the "abusive boy" point of view,
-Nini Conner, for her fabulous cover,
-Laurie Dennison, for the brilliant suggestions and the emails that lifted me up,
-Kristen Harmel and her critique group at the UNF writers conference, especially Allyson Richards and Eve Langrell,
-all the members of KipTaylorBooks, especially Jen Abbe, Hilary Blanchard, Tamara Brown, Julie Cutlip, Jessica and Jennifer deGroot, Kaitlin Gavrelis, Travis Grammer, Aimee Hutchison, Marney Kirk, Justin Robey, Bailey Wilhelm, Jonathan Williams, and Chrissy Wiskerchen,
-my peers at Columbia Writers Group: Grant Baker, Nicole Cross, Jenifer Michael, Sonja Thomas, Jessica Wilson, and especially Adam Schwartz,
-Ann Burke and her students at Baines Middle School,
-Michael Thorne, for cheerleading, private jokes, and computer skill,
-Valerie Allen, for her editing skills,
-my wonderful friends: Joyce Caldwell, Rosemary Gere, Chris Gibson, Carolyn Lorenz, Nancy Maider, Adele Merti, Lynn Pforr, and Julee Williams,
-thirty years of students, for great material and memories,
-my family: Tony, Erin, Maile, and Kai Talbert, Mike, Sacha, and Madison Taylor, Jordan Kroft, Matt, Alyssa, Alivia, Emalee, and especially Alex Free, Kara Cotsalas and Mark Rabinowitz, Victoria and Elizabeth Pontious,
-Gagi, for reading at least a bazillion drafts,
-Sebastian and Samson Taylor, my muses,
-and for taking care of me always, Philip Taylor.

About the Author

Kip Taylor loves young people. As a retired educator, working for thirty years with middle school students, Kip noted what made them such a highly discerning audience, and combines a love of the "middle child" with a love of literature.

Kip lives in Maryland during the summer and fall and in Florida during the winter and spring, a condition known as *snow-birding*. Kip enjoys traveling, grandchildren, Ravens football, reading, and playing endless fetch and tug-of-war games with the dogs.

You can reach Kip at the KipTaylorBooks Facebook page, or at ktaylor618@gmail.com.